Dear Bri

CAMINO TO LOVE

Enjoy your trip to northern Spain! Thanks for your support

YOLANDA ELSO-PONZO

Camino to Love
Copyright © 2023 by Yolanda Elso-Ponzo

All rights reserved. No part of this publication may be reproduced, distributed, or transmitted in any form or by any means, including photocopying, recording, or other electronic or mechanical methods, without the prior written permission of the author, except in the case of brief quotations embodied in critical reviews and certain other non-commercial uses permitted by copyright law.

Tellwell Talent
www.tellwell.ca

ISBN
978-0-2288-9230-4 (Hardcover)
978-0-2288-9229-8 (Paperback)
978-0-2288-9231-1 (eBook)

For my precious family and my cherished friends:
My community of love.

CHAPTER ONE

Lily cupped his sweaty, quivering hands. Breathing deeply to stop the queasiness, she parked herself in front of his chair. Their knees fused like sticky sugar.

"The police will find her."

Miguel's pallid face blended in with the sterile yellow walls of the comisaría. He said nothing, as his head rocked in rhythm with the rattling fan in the corner of the office. The moisture in the air enveloped them, as the sharp odour of alcohol drifted from the main reception area, overflowing with drunk partygoers. The street festival music mocked his anguish. "How can this be happening?"

Lily mulled over the same thought, as her watery eyes fixed on Miguel's wrist tattoo. Two days ago, his cutting words had ravaged her. It was over. Now, she brought comfort to his crushed spirit as they waited to complete the Missing Person's Report.

Her once in a lifetime trip to Spain had taken a cruel twist.

Lily sat hunched on the blemished parquet floor beneath her Pops's closet. Her beat-up grey sweatpants kept catching on the lifted planks. Warmth and familiarity reverberated through the damaged tiles. She could feel his presence, even though he had died last fall.

With their lease terminating at the start of May, cleaning up her father's belongings could no longer be delayed. The modest flat they shared for most of Lily's twenty-five years was simple but treasured. Leaving this home orphaned marked another devastating milestone in this challenging year.

Lily examined the peeling wallpaper inside the closet, concealing the crumbling surface. The once packed space now accommodated few items. The navy custodian's uniform that Pops wore proudly during the night shift at the bank, dangled like a mobile in a nursery. A single spike secured the horizontal clothes rail. Lily applauded the nail's tenacity in holding up the rod, despite limited support.

Her oldest friend, Jade, had cautiously agreed to help Lily purge. A morning of sorting had decluttered his room, but the smell of pine air freshener remained. So had the empty bottles of whisky buried between Pops's sneakers on the flimsy shoe rack. Jade had tried to quietly remove them earlier, but Lily uncovered her mission in the blue recycling box.

His weekend drinking was steady. Rubbing her slim legs, Lily could hear her father crooning his beloved drunken ABBA tune, "Tonight the super trouper lights are gonna find me/ Shining like the sun/ Smiling, having fun/ Feeling like a number one…" The corners of her mouth reluctantly turned up.

Jade sat on Pops's bed, watching Lily explore. She was not accustomed to any domestic chores. Her ballerina posture supported her curvy build. An Aegean blue Gucci tracksuit was Jade's cleaning uniform, easily afforded by her flourishing PR career. A pyramid of casual wear rested beside her. "Will Goodwill even take these hideous jeans? He had so many."

Rescued from her contemplation, Lily smirked back at her closest friend. "Most were cast-offs from a buddy at work who gained too much weight. I didn't realize he had so many T-shirts. What a hoarder!"

"Well, you certainly didn't inherit that trait from him, Ms. Organization!" Jade propped her chin and gawked at Lily.

"It's easy to stay tidy when you have fewer things to organize, Princess." Lily's wink was stained with a touch of resentment.

"My new personal assistant, Anita, keeps my life in perfect order." Jade stuck out her tongue in defiance.

Lily launched a charcoal slipper. Gracefully dodging to one side, Jade narrowly escaped the smelly projectile. The pile of clothes plunged off the bed. An eruption of laughter permeated the room. The tension Lily held broke loose. They were nine again; huddled inside Jade's treehouse, as her brother's army lofted mud balls at them.

"Ok, joker. Let's get serious. Goodwill closes at five today." Lily was ashamed to know their schedule so intimately. *At least this time I'm donating.*

Lily retrieved a dusty Nike shoebox from the closet. "Gross." The chalky air collected in the back of her throat, as she lifted the ripped lid.

"More running shoes?" Jade flung an armful of clothes back on the bed.

"I can't believe he kept these." Tears dripped on the cards that Lily removed from the box. Her friend intuitively clutched Lily's shoulder. Rainbow-hued sparkles floated through the air, as a parade of homemade cards marched out of the box.

"We made this monstrosity in Mrs. Garner's class, Lil. That was my final year in public school, before transferring to Hawthorne Private." Jade displayed a Father's Day card constructed in the shape of a turquoise tie.

Trying to subdue the throat lump, Lily smiled. "He howled when I gave it to him. When have you ever seen my Pops wearing a tie?" A beat-up sweatshirt would have been a more appropriate shape for his Father's Day card.

Her forehead wrinkled as she noticed a wedding picture. Jade plucked the photo. "He's wearing a tie here! So, 1980s! Daddy's second wife wore a frock like this. Look at your mother's puffy sleeves and oversized skirt. She resembles a child doing her First Holy Communion." Jade rattled her head.

"She was young. Fifteen years younger than Pops! How did they ever think it could work?" Pops looked radiant beside his pregnant young bride.

"I bet the sex was extraordinary." Jade bounced on the bed and gyrated her hips. Lily flung the matching slipper.

"You exhaust me, Jade." Lily kneaded her temples. Thinking about her mother was the real cause of her fatigue.

"On a serious note, you do get your beauty from her, Lil. You have her green eyes and youthful freckles."

"Whatever ... they would be the only gift I ever received from Véronique." Lily wrestled the photograph back and tossed it into the box. She had little time for this woman who walked away from her family when Lily was a child.

She drew a book that peeked out of the box. A frayed copy of *The Sun Also Rises* by Ernest Hemingway settled on Lily's lap. Jade examined the dark blue cloth cover with gold and silver lettering.

Slumping back onto the bed, Jade's analysis continued. "What a surprise! I assumed Pops only read the sports section."

Biting the inside of her cheek, Lily took a gulp. "It was my grandfather's book." Lily caressed the cover.

"Is it a first edition? Could be valuable." Her steel blue eyes flickered.

"It's not a first edition ... but it's priceless. Pops loved this novel." Lily leafed through the musty pages. She delighted in the perfume of old books. "If I remember correctly, it's about a group of friends, British and American expats, who travel to the Festival of San Fermín in Pamplona, Spain."

"Please don't bore me with another lecture, teacher." Jade hopped off the bed and headed to the kitchen.

"I *am* a teacher. I can't help myself." After graduating last June, Lily spent a frustrating year looking for a full-time teaching position.

The next round of interviews would hopefully secure a job for the coming fall.

As she caressed the book, a black and white photograph dropped out. Lily's face beamed with recognition. The book housed her grandfather's last remaining photograph. *How appropriate*! Taken during the Spanish Civil War in the 1930s, her lanky grandfather stands erect and grins, as a cigarette dangles from his mouth. He leans on a rifle with his left arm. His right drapes the shoulder of a shorter man, wearing spherical eyeglasses and a beret. This Spaniard saved his life and cemented a bond to Spain that fascinated her Pops. "Time for lunch?"

After gulping down leftover Pad Thai, the two friends got back to work. "Put the rest into the garbage." The trunk of Jade's SUV provided ample room for Pops's belongings. April drizzle coated the silver vehicle; the damp air drilled into Lily's bones. It was nippy, but the fertile smell of earthworms reminded her that spring would come soon. Toronto winters were too long and too grey. Lily craved sunshine.

She scooted back into the unassuming bungalow. "I think this lamp is in good shape. Someone could use it." Standing at the front door, she clutched the light fixture, anticipating a wisecrack from Jade that never landed.

Back inside, Lily combed her father's bedroom for any last-minute donations.

"Enough with playing the philanthropist! Naomi is doing my nails at six, Lil." Jade's voice projected through the flat from outside.

Lily scooped Pops's favourite hoodie and threw it in the direction of the Nike box. *I'm keeping this one.* The box tipped on impact, unveiling more treasures.

Lily lifted a bursting kraft envelope. Her father's scrawled cursive writing appeared on the front: *For my precious Lily Bear. Take the trip I never could.* The throat lump reawakened.

"All right. You can bring the decrepit lamp. But that's it!"

Oblivious to Jade's screeching, she ripped the seal. Her misty eyes overflowed as she thumbed the crammed five-, ten-, and twenty-dollar bills. A silky red scarf peered from beneath the pile. Lily instantly comprehended her father's request. With lamp and envelope in hand, she bolted outside.

The potent scent of orange spice perfume circulated in Jade's car. "What do you mean you can't take this trip?" The seatbelt felt rigid across Lily's chest as crumbled bills overflowed the box on her lap. The frosty leather seat would take some time to warm.

"Pops always had a fascination with Spain because my grandfather fought there and fell in love with the country. He fantasized about Hemingway's journey to the Festival of San Fermín but never followed through because he couldn't afford it, or his health prevented him from travelling." Lily straightened the bills as she envisioned her father, wearing the bright scarf, dancing around their tiny kitchen, describing the Running of the Bulls. "This was his dream, not mine, Jade." As these words left her mouth, the guilt set in. *I would love to do this for Pops.*

Jade's knuckles turned white as she gripped the steering wheel. "You are missing the obvious fact: he wanted you to go and has financed it, for once." Pops had consistently provided the basics for his only daughter. "Extras," like nice clothes and shoes, books, movie tickets, bus fare, and lunch money were Lily's responsibility.

"He would understand if I used this money to pay down my student loan." Lily closed the box and wiggled to ease her stiff legs. Her five years as a university student had left her in debt. "I will hopefully have a full-time teaching job in September. I'll be able to do some travelling in the future." Picking at her cuticles, she drew blood.

"When was your last vacation? Weekend camping doesn't count."

The sound of a European adventure charmed Lily. Unable to find work as a certified teacher, she had spent the last year juggling three part-time jobs. Her defeated eyes gazed out the tinted window.

"It would be reckless of me to take a trip with so many bills to pay! Besides, I have enough to cover the flight, but then what? I'll need money once I'm there." Lily nudged the power window switch to let in some air. A trip to Spain was such a luxury for a young person who kept her meagre savings in a Tim Horton's coffee tin.

"I know you will flatly refuse any money I might offer, but I have another solution." Lily considered her friend's plan, as she massaged cream onto her splintered hands. "What about a working vacation? I may have a connection at a school in Northern Spain."

Jade's proposal and the smiling face on the blue Goodwill sign calmed her nervous stomach. *Maybe I can go to Spain.*

CHAPTER TWO

Lily rolled her modest luggage into the narrow bedroom of the pensión on the first day of summer. The soft scent of bleach welcomed her to this humble guesthouse in Spain—her home for the next six weeks. The shared washroom facility across the hall reminded her of carefree days at university. She collapsed on the single bed adjoining the wall. Her hands rubbed against the brittle starchy sheets. The small saffron armchair at the foot of the bed would likely bear the weight of her gear. Lily spied a simple wash basin in the corner of the room. The awning window, the size of a pizza box, acknowledged the June breeze, as it knocked against the frame. The window shared the back wall with an ornate brass sconce. *This will work.*

Her exhausted eyelids finally surrendered. After the prolonged flight and train ride, Lily craved sleep. *Why didn't I allow Jade to upgrade me to business class?*

Lily's stubbornness often led to hardship.

Jade had already done so much to make this trip a reality. She introduced Lily to Fergus, the director of Alegría Language School. Having accepted a teaching position at his summer day camp, Lily could afford her stay in Pamplona. Jade had also agreed to join Lily for a few weeks, eager to explore Northern Spain.

With a smile on her face, Lily drifted off, thinking of her father. *I made it here, Pops!*

Groggy but refreshed, her first morning in Spain commenced. Lily bundled her wavy caramel hair into her signature ponytail, stretched her hamstrings, quads, calf muscles and darted outside. At home, she ran daily, untangling her thoughts, as her slender body navigated the familiar path. Today's jog required memorizing a new route and adjusting to the early morning heat.

Around the corner from the guesthouse was a broad avenue. Strollers, pedestrians, and dog walkers roamed without restraint. Lily grinned when she skillfully kicked back the black and white ball to the pint-sized football players, who waved zealously. The panadería propped open its door, flooding the air with the toasted, yeasty aroma of freshly baked bread. Lily's stomach rumbled but her legs kept pace, as she dodged the tiny puddles left behind by the imposing street-flushing trucks. The sun shimmered on the wet sidewalk.

Lily's eyes feasted on the pageantry. Vibrant garden patios, quaint shops, stately buildings, grandiose banks, ornamental fountains, elegant theatre facades, and imposing statues of former monarchs crossed her range of vision. Indebted to her high school education, Lily recalled many Spanish words. The sign for CASCO VIEJO led her to the medieval centre of the city but exploring this quarter of Pamplona would have to wait. She needed to shower before heading to school. Lily sprinted back in the direction of the pensión to get ready for the first day of teacher orientation week.

Close to the guesthouse, Lily's abdomen tightened. A cramp pierced her stomach. She halted the jog and slumped over to gasp. This rarely happened, but the lack of hydration and jet lag were a tricky combination.

"Ven, siéntate here." A gentle older woman directed Lily to a bistro chair outside a small café. A tall glass of water awaited. The affectionate woman stroked Lily's back as she gulped. Though she was a stranger, the gesture did not feel awkward.

"Thank you so much." Lily could feel her cheeks burn. "My name is Lily."

"Lily! Hello. I am Cristina. Sorry for my bad Ingles." Lily loved the way Cristina pronounced her name. It sounded like *Lee-Lee*, and her voice had a raspy character. "Maybe you run mucho? Sit, sit." Her manicured hand settled on Lily's shoulder. Cristina returned to watering the box planters, overflowing with yellow irises.

As she placed the empty glass on the table, Lily admired the brick exterior and arc-shaped window above the magenta door. An etched wooden sign CAFÉ MIISA hung above the entrance. "Is this your café?"

"Yes ... well, my familia's." Cristina looped her bronze hair behind her ear, revealing a dainty pearl earring.

"It's lovely. I wish I could stay, but I need to get back. Thank you for your help. Next time I'll walk here and have a coffee!" Lily's face shone in appreciation.

"Adiós. I happy to meet you." Lily vanished down the street, smiling back at this kind woman and her charming mistakes with English.

The bouquet of brewed coffee triggered Miguel's memory of happy days around the family kitchen table. He envisioned Papá scanning the newspaper, as Mamá reproached Miguel for pulling out Isabel's braid. This coffee was for his guests. A wistful stare dimmed his bronzed face. He cast aside a heap of unopened bills and plugged in the toaster.

Gazing at the window, he surveyed the patio and inhaled the crisp country air. The wind had blown the periwinkle recliner cushions onto the emerald grass. The chairs were jumbled against the teak bench, but Miguel had remembered to bring in the cactus plants that perched on the garden table. The wildflowers and songbirds appeared unruffled. Miguel would organize the yard ahead of the hospital visit.

The stone walls and dark wooden beams overhead remained from the original farmhouse—Miguel had resisted his sister's plan to renovate their grandparent's home. He was wary of upsetting the memories nested in the walls. Miguel argued a B&B should look rustic, while Isabel aspired to a fusion of old and new. She was correct, of course, and Miguel was now the benefactor of her vision. His lips pressed tight into a grimace, as he slowly dried the deep, white fireclay sink, and the arching stainless steel faucet.

"Good morning or should we say *buenos días*?" The Dutch guests rose early and appeared famished.

Smile, Miguel. He nodded at the vacationers. His straight full eyebrows were slightly furrowed. His sweeping eyelashes and brown eyes could not brighten his aloof expression. Miguel assembled the platter of cheeses and cold cuts, as his guests settled at the harvest table. Cherries, donut peaches, and yellow melon delivered colour to the white quartz counter of the kitchen island. Awaiting the arrival of the coffee, the tourists poured a goblet of freshly squeezed orange juice from the cobalt ceramic pitcher.

"Buenos días, Familia Janssen." The always peppy Elena barrelled through the front door of the B&B. "I am so sorry. The bakery was very busy this morning." Elena's chattiness permeated the kitchen. "Ria, I made sure to get you bollos suizos. Dunk this brioche into the café con leche. It's delicious." The market bakery was exceptional, but it fell short of Isabel's creations.

"Gracias, Elena." Miguel greeted her with the customary cheek kissing. A smile peeked out from the corners of his mouth.

"I hope you are going back to Pamplona tonight to watch the game with Antonio. You need some distractions, Miguel." Elena had worked at the B&B since they opened two years ago. When Miguel reduced her hours, as the hospital bills mounted, Elena remained unfailing in her loyalty to the family. Even her gregarious teenage children often rode their bikes to the inn and journeyed guests around their fabled town.

"Antonio won't let me off the hook today. But I'll drive back this evening from Pamplona, so you don't need to stay overnight." Elena's robust hands plumped the oversized pillows from the sectional in the common room. She wrapped an apron around her full figure and quickly swapped out her shoes.

"Have a good time, Miguel. Say hello to Isa for me." She flew up the stairs to gather the bedding.

The clinking of the cutlery against the plates suggested the guests were fond of the meal. "Can I offer you more coffee?" Miguel peered at his watch as he filed into the kitchen to gather fresh pastries for his Monday visit with Isabel, a fitting change from hospital food.

CHAPTER THREE

"Could you please call her one more time?" Lily gripped her wrist and admired the hotel receptionist's attire. Her navy and white polka dot blouse was bound together by a loose bow. The oversized belt that topped her pencil skirt accentuated her slim waist. Patent pumps completed the outfit. Lily's casual look seemed out of place, but she didn't mind. Unflinching, she twirled her silver teardrop earring, swivelled her peach tunic over her skinny jeans, and delighted at her white Converse sneakers.

"I am sorry. Your friend is not answering the phone. You may wait here in the lobby." Her petite hand motioned Lily towards the tufted velvet sofa. After a long first day at school, a rest was appealing.

From her cushy seat, she could see the sparkling antique chandelier and gilded mirror that greeted her at the entrance to the Gran Hotel La Perla. Only a five-star hotel from the nineteenth century would satisfy Jade.

Lily puzzled over the meeting time. *She did say 8:00 p.m., didn't she?* Her patience returned, as she recalled Jade blowing off her romantic trip to Lake Como with Ryan and springing into Lily's escapade. *She'll show up soon.*

Visitors strutted upon the immaculate marble floor of the boutique lobby. The vitality in the air was contagious. *I think I like working abroad.* Lily sensed a lightness in her chest.

When Fergus Paterson interviewed her, the summer director of Alegría Language School was adamant the program resembled camp for both kids and staff. Laughter and merriment invigorated the day's lesson-planning session. Sipping on sangría, Lily's rowdy team identified age-appropriate learning goals connected to the themes of "Space and Aliens," "Mad About Music" and "Zoo Friends." The school's name—*Joy*—had been wisely selected.

The elegant receptionist approached. "Excuse me, miss. Your friend would like to invite you to her room now." Thrilled for the night ahead, Lily scooted to the antique elevators.

The door to the room was open. "Jade?" Lily could hear the humming of the hair dryer. *This must be it.*

"I'm running a tad late, Lil. Make yourself comfortable." Jade bellowed as she styled her blond mane.

Lily plodded in and slapped her hands against her cheeks. *Wow*! She wandered through the lavish studio. The unmistakable scent of bergamot soap sailed out of the washroom and docked in the bedroom. The decor was very contemporary for a historic hotel. Muted neutrals tinted the two adjacent rooms, separated by a glass wall. The cognac oak flooring and recessed lighting delivered a glow to the suite, while the cool air offered a break from the sticky June evening. Lily stroked the buttery satin sheets. The sleek ash-grey headboard was somewhat hidden by the flock of layered cushions.

Equally lush was the living room. Warm wood paneling cradled the walls. The two wide leather armchairs commanded attention. Fancy shopping bags curled up to their legs. A glass table with a wrought-iron frame rested in the middle, shouldering an opulent bouquet of pink roses. Lily tiptoed towards the chalk-white balcony door, afraid to upset the splendid ambiance.

She drifted out. Greeted by the tepid breeze, her wide eyes peered over the railing to the street below, Calle Estafeta. From above, Lily spotted bars, souvenir shops, restaurants, and boutiques lining the narrow, cobbled road. Few people strolled tonight. Glued to television screens, the locals were captivated by the World Cup match: Spain versus Honduras. Lily had passed on the invitation for beer and footy with her colleagues from school. She had already arranged a date with her best friend, and Jade did not "do sports."

"There you are." Looking like a goddess and wearing a hooded bathrobe, Jade delivered an airtight hug. "Charming street, isn't it?"

Lily nodded. "It's probably one of the most famous in Pamplona! Especially during the Running of the Bulls, when they cross this stretch before reaching the bullring."

Jade extended her arms like a triumphant boxer. "Well, naturally. That's why I selected this hotel ... and Hemingway supposedly lodged here in room 217." Lily's jaw dropped. "I pleaded with you to stay with me, remember?"

Lily appreciated Jade's generosity but usually turned it down. Her father's vast real estate holdings and Jade's lucrative PR firm afforded her an affluent lifestyle. Lily's intense envy of Jade's universe had disappeared in high school, when she started working part-time and was finally able to provide for her own "extras." Since then, a thirst for self-sufficiency had shaped Lily's nature.

"I'm staying at a cute place." Composing her best puppy dog eyes, Lily stared at Jade. "But I will definitely come here to see the Running of the Bulls."

Roaming back into the living room, Jade reached into her coral Prada tote and tossed Lily a key card. "In case you need an upgrade from the convent." Thrusting her shoulders back and chest forward, Lily curtsied as she snagged the card.

Miguel spotted Dani waving them into the Bodegón. "I saved you a table, stranger." Miguel leapt to bear hug his dear friend and owner of the bar. Dani's embrace was solid for a man in his early seventies. His few strands were greying but his hazel eyes remained youthful.

"¡Tanto tiempo sin verte!" He was right—Miguel's last visit to the tapas bar had been months ago. His austere face softened, soothed by the familiar terrain. The hams still hung from the low ceiling beams and the countertop of the bar was packed with delicious pintxos. As a child, his father had ordained Miguel into his sacred football rituals. Important matches were eternally observed at the Bodegón.

Miguel's best friend, Antonio, hauled out the wood chair. His square-shaped eyeglasses slid over his nose. He had grown a full beard since their last visit. Antonio's keys dropped on the solid table, as Dani brought them two beers and two Ibérico ham sandwiches.

"You need a bit of sun, amigo, but you look great!" Miguel's braided leather bracelet hung low on his wrist as he placed his hand on Antonio's shoulder and silently mouthed *thank you*. Miguel's gloominess had alienated many friends, but not Antonio. He remained loyal through it all.

Biting into the crusty bun, Miguel studied the image on the television screen. The confident faces of the Honduran football team were spotlighted as their national anthem reverberated Ellis Park Stadium in Johannesburg. The bar was bristling with anticipation for a Monday night. The World Cup football match was about to commence. As the Euro champions, the Spanish team had endured an embarrassing loss in their first group stage match to Switzerland. Triumph today was critical. Miguel also needed a victory.

Dani returned to their table, took off his soiled apron and plunked himself. "How is Isabel doing?"

Looking at his beer, Miguel's racing pulse returned. "Not well. Her spinal cord injury is incomplete so she may recover, but her progress has been very slow. The brain injury isn't helping things."

Dani's sorrowful eyes betrayed his optimistic words. "The clínica at the university is one of the best in Europe. Give her time. Isabel is a fighter." Miguel spied Antonio looking critically at his father's dear friend.

"Ok, guys, let's focus on the game."

Antonio's interruption thankfully lightened the weight of the conversation. Relieved, Miguel had a swig of his beer and witnessed

David Villa score the first goal. The Bodegón exploded with joy. *Maybe this will be a good night.*

The Plaza del Castillo or Castle Square was steps away from Jade's hotel. The narrow streets of the Old Town emerged from this pedestrian nerve centre. Arcaded on all sides, terraces and cafés lined the perimeter of the square—this was the playground for the characters in *The Sun Also Rises*. In the centre, a blue-domed kiosk attracted the attention of onlookers. After a carefree stroll through the crammed roads of the Casco Viejo, Lily and Jade rested on a copper-coloured bench.

"I adore the school. The team Fergus assembled is excellent. There are two teachers from the UK who taught at Alegría last year, one from the US, and three from Australia. The rest are Spanish." Lily leaned back and cradled her knees to her chest. "I can't wait for the kids to start next week."

"My nightmare! I have no patience for little people." Jade rattled her head, as she took out a new scarlet lace fan. "You haven't put in enough time with brats. You grew up an only child with no cousins. That's why you can tolerate them."

As a child, Lily pretended her few stuffed animals were siblings and cousins. Spending "time with brats" was her dream.

"More importantly, what's your assessment of Fergus?" A flush crept across Jade's face.

Lily abruptly swung to the right to examine her friend's embarrassed look. "You like him!"

Looking away, Jade reluctantly conceded. "For the three summers we vacationed at my uncle's villa near Edinburgh, I was infatuated with him. Sadly, I was overlooked, what with the seven-year age gap. I was a mere teenager, and he was a potent man in his mid-twenties."

"And what about Ryan?" Jade's on-again, off-again relationships were difficult for Lily to keep track of.

Shrugging her shoulders, Jade looked unconcerned. "We are on a break."

"If that's the case, I think Fergus is a wonderful person, and his Scottish accent is divine—but he isn't exactly your *usual* type, Jade."

Sitting upright, Jade's eyebrows squished together. "And what might that type be?"

Lily leaned in and whispered, "GQ cover model, like Ryan."

Jade rolled her eyes. "What about you, Reverend Mother? Do you still have a type? You barely dated this last year."

Directing her gaze at the base of the light pole, Lily had more critical matters to contemplate. "I have no time for a relationship right now."

Jade jumped in before Lily could complete her thought. "You have the entirety of next year mapped out, since you landed that teaching job for the fall. Where is your spontaneity? Life is messy, darling."

Lily rejected the thought. What was wrong with looking forward to some stability and security in her life?

Jade bounced off the bench and yanked on Lily's ponytail. "A summer fling would do us both some good." Not convinced, Lily followed Jade through the square.

CHAPTER FOUR

San Nicolás Street, just off the Plaza del Castillo, billowed with people.

"What's going on?" Jade skirted a group of football devotees, as they raised wine glasses, toasting their team's momentum.

"It must be halftime." Lily tugged Jade's arm as they shimmied their way into the closest eatery. Standing by the wooden bar, Lily's mouth watered. The multi-levelled display counter was overflowing with what locals called "pintxos"; small snacks served on bread and held by a cocktail toothpick. They ordered swiftly by pointing at the mushroom croquettes, pepper balls, egg and potato omelette, shrimp stacks, fried brie with tomato jam, and chorizo.

"Dos cañas, por favor." A satisfied grin emerged as Lily glanced at her friend. Jade slowly lowered her head, unaware of Lily's confidence with the language. Two small glasses of draft beer were gingerly delivered by a pleasant older man, followed by a train of pintxos.

As the second half of the match commenced, standing space along the bar shrunk. Jade followed the sign for the restroom, as Lily finished the last morsel of bread. Her eyes set on the television screen behind her—maybe she could catch a few minutes of play before Jade inevitably dragged her out.

The bar suddenly erupted as the Spanish team scored its second goal. Fisted arms thrust into the air, as the patrons chanted, "Olé! Olé! Olé! Olé!" Immersed in the party, Lily sang along.

A clueless Jade returned as the goal was replayed. "Got it! The red jersey guys must be Spain, right?" The young bartender, wiping the counter, snickered at this dazed turísta. Giving a quick shake of the head, Jade dragged Lily in the direction of the seating area, instead of the door. She stealthily pulled out two barstools from the snug corner of an occupied table.

"Can we join you?" When Jade flashed her sparkling Hollywood smile, who could resist? Lily's mouth opened but no words emerged. *Does Jade want to watch the game?* This baffling thought was erased, as she peered over at the two attractive men at the other end of the table.

"Of course, please sit. Do you have enough room?" The bearded man scootched over, towards his serious-looking companion.

"Thank you. My name is Jade, and this is Lily."

"Hello. My name is Antonio, and this is Miguel." A cobweb of handshaking formed.

"Four cañas, por favor." Jade was a quick study.

Miguel lobbed a pack of Marlboros on the table, plotting his escape. The blonde's chatter was unwavering, as was Antonio's patience with her endless questions. She had treated them to a round—which was hospitable—but the *game* was on!

"Wasn't that offside?" The cute friend was at least attentive to the match. "I think the linesman was sleeping."

Antonio nodded in solidarity.

Rolling back his stiff shoulders, Miguel rose. "Be right back." Rounding the corner of their table, he lunged forward to pick up the cigarette pack he had left behind. His elbow set in motion a beer tsunami that splashed onto the cute one's chest.

"Oh dear!" yelled the blonde. "Hand me those serviettes, quickly." She frantically patted the flowing beer. "Go back to La Perla and change out of those clothes, Lily."

"It's not a big deal, really." Lily appeared calmer than her hysterical friend.

"I'm very sorry." Miguel dashed towards the bar. Dani, who must have seen the incident, chuckled, as he flung a towel with cold water and dish soap to Miguel. Returning, Lily was absent from the table. Miguel did a double take. "Did she return to the hotel?"

"No, she is far too stubborn to do the sensible thing. She's outside, drying off." The blonde's bitter smile reminded Miguel of Señorita García, before escorting him to the principal's office.

Miguel discovered Lily out front. Leaning, the foot of her bent leg gripped the brick wall. As she fluttered her blouse, tugging on the hem, her slender bare midriff was visible.

"You can use this to clean up." Miguel turned over the towel.

"It's almost dry; but thank you. It cooled me off!" Her kind almond-shaped green eyes sparkled under the glow of the streetlight. "You should go back and finish watching the game." Lily dabbed her tunic in a circular motion. "That should do it." Miguel collected the towel and raced back into the bar.

Replacing the beer he had tumbled ranked above the match. Back outside of the Bodegón, he delivered the frosted drink and smiled. "I owe you this." Miguel removed the cigarettes from the back pocket of his jeans.

Lily drew the glass to her full lips and sipped the foam off the top. "Gracias." Her face lit. "Your English is very good."

Fidgeting with the pack, he looked away. "I studied in London a few years ago. It was an intensive course." Those months away were clouded by guilt. Miguel let out a deep breath.

"As a teacher, it sounds to me like their program was excellent. I wish my Spanish was that strong."

Miguel appreciated the compliment. "I use my English every day at my family's B&B."

"You must meet so many interesting people. Is the B&B in Pamplona?"

He played with the cigarette pack, shaking his head. "No. It's in a very pretty town, just twenty minutes by car from here."

Lily playfully shrugged her shoulders. Tugging at her ear, she leaned into Miguel. Pointing at the Marlboro pack, she whispered. "Are you going to have one?" Her cheekiness was angelic.

"No. I don't smoke." They both chuckled at the absurdity. "I meant to say, I used to smoke, but I promised my father I'd stop." Speaking to this stranger felt effortless.

"So ... holding the pack prevents you from actually smoking?" Lily's ponytail whirled to the right, as she tilted her head.

Lifting his chin, Miguel agreed. "Precisely."

Raising her glass to commend him, Lily momentarily locked eyes with Miguel. "Your father must be very proud of you."

"I hope so ... he passed three years ago from lung cancer." He looked away, rubbing his chest.

A pained stare remodelled her face. "I'm so sorry, Miguel."

"Since I was a kid, he brought me to the Bodegón to watch all of the important matches."

Lily's tender eyes soothed him. "You must feel close to him when you're here."

Miguel nodded. The memories housed at the bar were a great comfort to him.

"I understand this feeling, Miguel. I lost my father last year." Staring at her feet, she bit her lower lip.

Complicit in grief, Miguel momentarily gripped her soft hand. "It gets easier with time, Lily, but you always carry the loss with you."

Lily broke the lingering silence and sombre mood. "My visit to Pamplona is thanks to my father. I'm taking the holiday he always dreamed about but left unfinished." The brightness returned to her delicate face.

"Your trip will need to be very special, then." Miguel ran his hand through his sable hair.

Their conversation was interrupted by a deafening roar. Miguel's joy soared watching the fans flooding out of the bar. Spain had won the match. Miguel observed Antonio and the blonde, caught in the current of celebration.

He dropped his head to Lily's ear and shouted above the chanting. The scent of beer, infused with her coconut shampoo, reminded Miguel of a day at the beach. "I enjoyed chatting with you." Angling towards Antonio, he squeezed her shoulder, and nodded farewell. "Adiós, cariño."

Football fans hijacked the city that evening. Lily's open window welcomed in more drunken singing than fresh air. The noise from outside was a minor irritant. Recalling the night's conversation with Miguel, was the true cause of her insomnia. Meeting charming and attractive men was not a unique experience but feeling such a strong connection with a perfect stranger was. Miguel had experienced the unique emptiness that she had felt, since last fall. When he squeezed her hand, she felt secure and understood: two emotions that had rarely visited Lily this last year.

Slipping out of bed, she thumped the window shut and pulled a mini dictionary out of her backpack. Skimming through the pages, she arrived at *cariño*: "*[noun] 1. love, affection, fondness. 2. darling.*" Floating back into bed, she buried her flushed cheek against the pillow.

The biting breeze accelerated Lily's stride. It was a chilly morning. With her new route established, she jogged, absorbed in planning her Tuesday. The "To Do" list was almost complete now that her lesson was planned. She required multicoloured recycled paper for the balls and magnets to assemble the word wall. Her selection of an introductory game called "Snowball Fight," prompted a rush of teasing by her colleagues. *Of course, the Canadian would choose to demonstrate this activity!* Her smile widened.

Shock replaced Lily's bright spirit, as she approached Cristina's coffee shop. Glass littered the patio. The window, adjacent to the magenta door, lay shattered. Lily gathered the larger fragments, as the café door swung open.

"No worry, please. I will clean this, Lily." An animated Cristina glided the wooden broom expertly, collecting the tiny shards into the black dustpan. Lily carried on, touched that her name had been recalled, after meeting Cristina only once.

Wrinkling her brow, she rubbed her hand on her bare leg, testing for glass splinters. "What happened?"

"No sé … maybe too much fiesta last night?" Cristina filled the last dustpan and waved Lily in.

How can she be so calm?

Inside the cozy café, the slate floors were free of debris. Two small tables bordered the brick wall. Apricot wildflowers filled the decorative bud vases. Towards the back, a sandy granite counter displayed a cash register and pastry dishes with glass-domed covers. Three frosted conical pendant lights illuminated the busy alcove. A small sink, espresso maker, and juicer lined the back wall. Above, Lily admired the seashells dotting the space, in the shape of angel wings, bubbles, figs, buttons, and turbans. "I take shells at the playa. Please sit. ¿Un café con leche?"

Lily nodded, as the gurgling song of the coffee machine echoed. The rounded back of the chair braced her perfectly as she stirred the brew. Cristina sprinkled sugar crystals from a paper sachet.

"You're not upset about this?" Lily's eyes widened, as she shifted to stare at the busted window.

"No. Windows are no importante—*people* are importante. I can fix this." Despite her words, Cristina's kind eyes looked troubled. Her shoulders dropped, as her spoon ladled the froth clinging to the bottom of her mug.

"A good point." Lily nervously twirled a strand of loose hair.

"¡Basta! No sad face." Cristina grabbed the cups and headed to the sink. "You see the game last night?" Her voice was buoyant.

A smile crept back onto her ivory face, as she draped the dishcloth over her shoulder.

"Some of it; I did hear the celebrations, all over the city. Congratulations!" Lily's cheeks glowed. Remembering game night, only one image vividly surfaced.

CHAPTER FIVE

Miguel's foot braced the door of the shop as he patiently waited for his niece to mope through. The magical-sounding door chime acknowledged the new patrons but received no attention from the drifting girl.

"¡Hombre! Two times in one week. I am a fortunate man." Antonio rose from his desk at the back of Arco Íris bookstore. Miguel sidestepped the giant puzzle pieces scattered on the splashy animal print rug. His niece waved at Antonio as she scooped a magazine from the neon yellow spinner and flopped onto the aquamarine bean bag chair. Miguel shrugged his heavy shoulders. "It's ok. Just let her be." He embraced his steadfast mate, lightly slapping his unshaven face.

Miguel forced a bubbly voice. "So, the beard is permanent?"

"I think I'll keep it for the summer." Antonio gently stroked his face.

"Until the boss comes back and decides whether or not *she* likes it?" Miguel relished the taunting. Antonio shook his head and slumped back into his well-worn chair.

"I came to see my niece and thought we'd treat you to lunch." Miguel's former life, before the accident, appeared for a moment.

"I wish I had known. Lucas didn't make it in today." Antonio leaned forward to gather a stack of documents.

"Too busy being a playboy last night?" Miguel had no charitable words—his hostility for Lucas had been slowly brewing over the past year. "Another time." He forced a smile, cloaking his disappointment.

Settling into a swivel chair wrapped in a furry unicorn cover, Miguel caught sight of a glossy brochure topping a mountain of papers on the corner of the desk, "Scope: Communications & Marketing."

Antonio predicted the trailing question. "This is Jade's company. She came by this morning."

Raising his eyebrows, Miguel thumbed through the folder. "Oh … the blonde from last night? I'm telling Beatriz!"

Antonio shook his head and laughed. "You know it's not like that. She came by to offer me some free advice on branding and putting the catalogue online. Jade is very knowledgeable."

"And very voluptuous!" Miguel teased Antonio, wagging his finger.

"And very persistent … she was all over me at the Bodegón and doesn't accept rejection very well. After last night, I'm surprised she still came by to help me!"

"Maybe she hasn't really given up?"

Firing back, Antonio boosted his chest and fixed his eyes on Miguel. "You should talk, amigo. You disappeared with the petite one for most of the second half!"

Miguel's face brightened. "We had a very sincere conversation." He propelled his body off the soft chair and walked towards the colourful shelving cushioning the back wall. Miguel pawed the book spines, avoiding his friend's inquisitive eyes.

"And?"

"And … nothing, Antonio. They are rich visitors passing through."

Orienting his glasses, Antonio let out a frustrated sigh.

Miguel's niece appeared and headed towards the door.

"I'll let you get back to work … I think my little partner is hungry." Anxious to bypass a lecture on the healing properties of dating, Miguel turned to face the door. "See you at the game?"

Antonio waved and nodded. "Looking forward to it."

The instructional kitchen at school was groomed to host the dinner bash, celebrating the end of the teacher orientation week. Lily had volunteered for the clean-up crew, which gave her time to finish assembling her classroom.

The smell of crayons, scented erasers, and sharpened pencils pacified Lily, like the essence of eucalyptus at a spa. She stood in a wide stance, fists on hips as she surveyed the room. Student desks were corralled in the shape of a horseshoe. Anchor charts with grammar lessons and inspirational posters hung at an appropriate height. The Reading Corner sign had been nimbly crafted using travel magazines collected at Barajas Airport, Madrid. Whimsical letters trimmed the empty bulletin boards. The welcome banner dangled, creating a floral canopy in the centre of the classroom.

Borrowed staff room plants sat along the base of the enormous windows, opposite the interior courtyard, but the glass wall looked empty. Sitting on the carpet with her faithful scissors, Lily began cutting out the land masses from an old map of the world. She skillfully pasted the continents on the glass window. Large letters formed the sign above the map: HOME IS WHERE THE HEART IS. *Much better!*

"There's the lass." Fergus and Jade strolled in, as Lily collected the clippings scattered on her lap. "I can't believe you already labelled the cubbies with the pupils' names!" Fergus's smile widened. "The classroom looks terrific, Lily."

Flipping her hair back, Jade winked. "Splendid job!"

Twisting her mouth to one side, Lily was not convinced. "Fergus, I will need more pillows and books for the Reading Corner and paint for our handprint mural."

"Aye, but that can plainly wait until Monday. We've come to fetch you—the Friday soiree is about to begin."

After a delicious dinner, Jade's glassy eyes focused on the director as he fraternized with the staff. Lily had her eyes on Jade. "So, you're glad you came?"

Lily's elbow ricocheted off Jade's toned arm.

"Well … yes. The invitation to dine at a sterile school cafeteria was unappealing, but the venue is much improved." A sly grin crossed Lily's face.

Scanning the kitchen, Lily congratulated her Alegría kin. "*All* of my colleagues have done a great job with the transformation." The central demonstration island held the bottles Trevor and Harper had decanted. The Aussie sisters, Charlotte and Ella, blissfully deejayed the event from the mobile cart, while the Spanish contingent of Ramón, Julia, and Mateo had organized the savoury meal on the expansive counters lining the side wall. The dinner was an incredible success.

Bobbing to "TiK ToK," the woozy faculty bellowed, "Don't stop, make it pop/DJ, blow my speakers up …"

Teased as he scaled the step stool, the director shook his elastic hips. Hoisting his glass, Fergus's rosy cheeks clashed with his ginger goatee. "I want to thank everyone for their enthusiasm and hard work, this week. With a record number of wee ones coming this summer, the solid reputation of the school has grown. Enjoy your bevvies everyone and see you next week!"

Lily joined Pablo and Joe for a dishwashing party. The two hours flew, thanks to the multiple sinks and the red wine spell. Lily led the clean-up crew as they burst into song when Lady Gaga's "Bad Romance" blasted through the speaker. Exacting a thundering ovation from those able to stand, it was a fitting end to the festivities.

Tilting her wobbly head back and looking upwards, Jade snapped, "Are you done yet? Fergus wants to take us out." Securing the leather strap of her purse to rest across her chest, Lily shook her head furiously.

She caressed Jade's shoulder, as a sister would. "You don't need *me* there. Go and have a great time."

"I agree, but he insists on *you* coming." Breathing deeply, Lily followed Jade outside.

Strolling along the bustling Plaza del Castillo, Fergus and Jade reminisced about summers past at the Fringe Festival. Muddled in their stories, Lily navigated the trio towards San Nicolás Street, knowing the World Cup game against Chile had just wrapped up.

Miguel and Antonio dipped back in their chairs, crossed their legs, and boosted their feet on the handrail of the wrought-iron balcony. Dani's tiny flat above the Bodegón granted asylum from the hoopla below. The ruby-red pacharán twirled around the ice in Miguel's snifter, as a flutter of anise infused the air. Clinking their glasses to the home team, the berry liqueur seesawed, like their game-time nerves.

Unshielded from the blaring music of the street, Antonio's feet tapped along. "What a game! I think your niece enjoyed it too."

"She did. It's in her blood. Her Abuelo would be so proud." Miguel's chest tightened. His father was ever present at the Bodegón.

"Their first-place standing means they won't have to play Brazil in the next round." Antonio rubbed his hands together, feeding off the energy in the air.

Temporarily doting on the victory, Miguel wished he didn't need to return to the B&B. Releasing his legs, he leaned his chest on the handrail. Toying with his cigarette pack, he observed the celebration below.

Squinting to better focus, Miguel spotted her golden locks and lean arms around a muscular companion. *Jade.* His pulse quickened as Miguel scanned her vicinity, looking for Lily. After a drawn-out search, his defeated eyes abandoned the mission.

Slapping Antonio's legs, Miguel shook his head. "You were telling me the truth about your blonde friend! Look." Stretching his legs, he sauntered, fronting Antonio's chair.

Peering over the balcony, Antonio raised his eyebrows and smirked. "That must be her boyfriend, Ryan, who was in Italy this month. She certainly got over me quickly! Looks like they reconciled."

Bobbing on the soles of his feet, Miguel leaned his back on the railing. "You know a great deal about your 'friend's' personal life, don't you?" The ribbing was short-lived.

"Looks like *your* friend is there too."

Miguel froze. "No …she's not."

"It looks like she was inside the bar. You can't miss the ponytail." Guardedly, Miguel pivoted and latched on to the handrail.

It *was* Lily! His eyes zeroed in as she entered a circle of people performing the Waka Waka dance. Her limber waist pulsated side to side, precisely in sync with her praying hands. The gentle popping of her chest was accompanied by her arms flipping upwards. *Shakira would be proud.*

As the chums journeyed off, Miguel's eyes followed the bouncing ponytail.

Antonio jumped, spanning his arms out wide. "Let's go say hello."

Emerging from the trance, Miguel tilted his head. "No. They are down the street by now. Besides, I need to take my niece home. I'm sure Dani needs a break from this last hour of babysitting."

Persisting, Antonio dared eye contact. "You are a dimwit! I bet she came here to find you."

Allowing a slight smile, the remark melted Miguel's tight chest. "Another time. Enjoy the weekend, Antonio." Straying to the staircase, his car keys jingled softly.

CHAPTER SIX

"Please choose one group leader for each station. This person will read aloud the recipe for the banana-chocolate chip muffins and make sure each step is done correctly." The rambunctious cohort of ten-year-olds had lost the shyness of the first day at school, by noon.

The little bakers slipped on the black and white aprons, remodelling the kitchen into a checkerboard. The match commenced briskly, as did the airing of complaints.

"Miss Harrison, Carmen isn't listening to me."

"What does *sift* mean?"

"When can *I* stir the flour, Miss Harrison?"

Lily circulated, inspecting the controlled mayhem. "Remember to speak English."

Turning to face the back wall, she spotted Amaya seated against the corner with her head between her knees. Lily joined the upset student, squatting to the carpet. After a few minutes of stillness, she whispered, "What's wrong?"

Amaya shook her head, as her chestnut bob cascaded.

"Can you look at me for a moment?" The girl cautiously lifted her head, exposing her large watery eyes. "I'm sorry you are having a bad day, Amaya. Do you want to tell me what's wrong?" The child shook her head.

Lily placed her hand on Amaya's shoulder. "I know what might help."

Lily bee-lined to the worktables and returned with a stainless-steel bowl, two bananas, and a potato masher. "Your group told me it was your job to prepare the bananas."

Wiping her eyes, Amaya sat up, nimbly peeled back the skin, and smashed the bananas with the power of a carpenter brandishing a hammer.

Lily watched Amaya march back to her group, bowl in hand, but she was hesitant to engage. *It's a start.*

Lily's relief was cut short by a high-pitched tattle. "Miss Harrison, Pedro is eating the chocolate chips!"

In the midst of this craziness, Fergus sheepishly poked his head into the kitchen. "Sorry about last night, Lily. Didn't mean to leave you stranded."

Displaying her amusement, she granted a slow nod and walked towards the door holding what was left of Pedro's bag of chocolate chips. "I made it back safely. Don't worry … Did you?"

Fergus shook his flushed face and chuckled. "Barely! The lass is demanding." Raising her hand, Lily terminated the conversation. Fergus bowed his head and disappeared behind the door.

"Would you like me to save you a muffin?" Projecting, Lily's yell caught Fergus.

"Aye."

Gently, he leaned over, kissing her pale cheeks. "Take care, Isa." Antonio clasped Isabel's hand as Miguel cloaked his shoulder, ushering the visitor to the door. "Next Monday, I'll bring your favourite chocolate."

The corners of her mouth slightly twisted upwards, but her gaze remained on the window. "That would be nice, Antonio."

At the entrance, the friends embraced. "One day at a time, amigo." This mantra had been Miguel's unwilling companion for the last six months.

"You're right. It's just hard to see Isabel this way."

Mustering a smile, Miguel retreated to his sister's room. He was fully acquainted with the subtle squeaking of the air exchanger and the antiseptic lemon tang filling the space. The wheel of her chair rested against the panel beneath the picture window of her hospital room. Isabel's stoic brown eyes tracked the action outdoors, as she spoke to Miguel. "It was nice to see Antonio. I wish I was having a better day." Her poor mental health competed boldly with her physical injuries.

"When he comes back with the chocolate, it will be a better day." Miguel winked at his sister, whose fondness for sweets had survived the car accident. No reaction. Isabel was engrossed by the activity in the parking lot below. "Dr. Ortiz says you are making some progress with your physiotherapy."

"I guess ... Dealing with the pain is difficult." Her trembling voice plowed over his fake smile. Smoothing his hand along the leg of his jeans, Miguel shifted topics.

"The B&B is fully booked for the summer. Your outside patio area is a hit with the guests." Her furrowed eyebrows appeared to release. "Javier is coming soon to install the first-floor ramps." Miguel counted down the days until Isabel's discharge from the hospital.

"Summer in the country sounds wonderful." Tilting her face to better absorb the natural light, Isabel propelled the chair back and pointed to the Arco Íris bag. "Don't forget the books for my girl. I will call her an hour later tonight—I have an extra session of acupuncture today."

Kissing her forehead, Miguel snapped up the parcel and departed.

A late Wednesday night was to blame for Lily's drowsiness and stiff muscles. Jade's excursion to the Guggenheim Museum in Bilbao with Fergus had freed up her time after school to finish the superhero outfits. The red, blue, and yellow plastic tablecloths were transformed into bright capes. Lily extended her arms, as her gratified eyes inspected the project. Skipping her morning jog was out of the question even though her body pleaded otherwise. She had an important muffin delivery.

Locating Cristina sweeping the patio outside the café, Lily drew near for a brief stopover. The potted blossoms wafted tangerine and musk into her sleepy lungs.

"Buenos días." Cristina propped the broom and embraced Lily. The CLOSED sign hung on the magenta door and the window had been repaired.

Fondly, Lily handed over a battered paper bag. "I brought you some muffins. These were my father's favourite." Her class had made them a few days ago, but Lily had stored these in an airtight container.

"Thank you. You are very generosa." Cristina affectionately patted Lily's arm before retreating inside. "I make coffee." Lily checked her watch as she kneaded the back of her neck.

"We sit outside, okay?" Entrusting Lily with the steamy café con leche, the two women mingled alongside the dewy flowers and brilliant daylight of the patio. Popping open the oil-stained bag, Cristina's hand lifted the treat to her mouth and nibbled the muffin top. "Muy bueno. Banana goes with chocolate very good. Your father is right."

Lily pictured Pops devouring two muffins before his tea hit the kitchen table. Reminiscing rekindled the glow on her face. "He loved my baking. That's the one thing I *can* do in the kitchen."

Cristina swabbed her chocolate smeared lips. "What happened to him?" Her kind eyes remedied the ache in Lily's chest.

"He died last year. Pops had a weak heart but a loyal devotion to whisky." Cristina paused as she placed her hand on Lily's knee.

"Lo siento mucho. My José died too, but he is here." Resting her weathered hand over her heart, Cristina glanced at her gold wedding band. "And Mamá?"

Gripping the coffee cup, Lily sighed. "I haven't seen her since my tenth birthday. She left us to start a new life in Quebec." Véronique had promised to have Lily visit her every summer, but the invitation never arrived. The frequency of the phone calls also diminished until no contact was the norm.

Shaking her head, Cristina's mouth sagged. "This is no right," she blurted.

"I'm focussing on the future, now. I have a full-time teaching job in September and when I get back home to Toronto, I'll be looking for a new apartment. Things are going to change for me this year." *They have to.*

Cristina's face brightened as she clutched Lily's hand. "This is good news!"

Noticing the time on her watch, she vaulted to her feet. Wishing Cristina a wonderful day, Lily scooted back to the pensíon to get ready for school.

The bulging backpack, that morning, grazed Lily's shoulder blade, as she sped along the sidewalk to Alegría Language School. Her champagne floral skirt fluttered, as the chime of her colourful bangles harmonized with each step. Clinging onto the garment bag, she glanced at her watch repeatedly. Droplets of sweat shimmered along her forehead.

Lily's brain raced over the morning lesson. She had displayed the hero word mats and the writing prompt pages, yesterday, after she photocopied the Superhero Identity worksheets. Claudia, the student monitor, would be recruited to lend a hand in dressing the superheroes before the oral presentations. Lily released a deep breath, as she approached the school.

Across the street, an alluring man waved as he called out. "Lily?" Slowing her pace, she observed the stranger rest his sunglasses in his tousled hair. Frozen momentarily, Lily's mouth fell open. "It's Miguel. We met the other night."

Regaining her poise, Lily's wide-open eyes channelled her confusion. "Of course! Hi, how are you?" Crossing the road, his indigo blue T-shirt hugged his chest.

As they shared the two-kiss salutation, Miguel's sweet citrus cologne swept over her. "I went by the Bodegón last Friday night, but I guess you had already left. We arrived after the game had finished."

Redness crawled across Miguel's cheeks. "I'm sorry I missed you."

Unhappy with the hour on her watch, Lily scrubbed a hand along her face. "I hate to be rude, Miguel, but I need to get to work."

Raising his eyebrows, he steadied his firm hand on Lily's bare arm. "I understand." His magnetic smile pacified the tension. "I'll make sure to save a table for you at the Bodegón for Saturday's game. Okay?"

"Wonderful!"

Unlocking eyes, Lily soared to school. *What a beautiful start to the new month of July.*

CHAPTER SEVEN

Miguel thumped the car door, tucking his keys in the pocket of his tan cargo pants. He surveyed the planters on the balcony—the surge of red geraniums needed watering. He approached the tastefully dressed couple in the gravel driveway of the B&B.

"Hello. Where are you off to?"

Professors at the University of Toulouse, the Morneau couple faithfully vacationed in Spain, every summer. "Good morning, Miguel! Short jaunt over to Pamplona. It's the A-12 we take, correct?"

Nodding, Miguel lightly tapped the hood of his white Renault. "Yes! You'll be there in twenty minutes, even with the Friday traffic. Be sure to visit the Museo de Navarra. Safe travels!"

Miguel collected the breakfast plates as he crossed the patio. Plucking a sweet bun from the pastry stand, he reclined on the kitchen counter, riffling through the mail, humming the song of the summer. The invoice from the hospital halted the tune. His brain turned to calculate expenses instead.

Heaving a mound of towels, Elena released the laundry basket and flopped onto the kitchen chair. "You got back from Pamplona quickly." She blotted the sweat from her forehead with a linen handkerchief. "I ran into Susana's father yesterday." Dropping the bills, Miguel focussed on the ceramic tile at his feet. "He asked about you."

Folding his arms on his chest, Miguel let out a sigh. "I guess I should stop by their place."

Elena fanned the hankie. "You were Susana's boyfriend for two years, Miguel. I'm sure a visit would help as they grieve her sudden death."

Head tilted, Miguel's chest tightened as he thought of his ex-girlfriend. "You know it's not that simple."

"You're right." Like a favourite aunt, she got up and parked her sturdy arm around Miguel, shaking him, and propping his chin with her bleach-scented hand.

Sitting back, Elena voluntarily changed the topic. "Are you certain about the time off? I can visit my brother in September, when Barcelona is less busy."

His eyes flashed sternly. "Elena … it's for a few days. No one deserves a break more than you. I'll be fine." Opening the dishwasher, Miguel stacked the dishes, still lukewarm from the cycle.

"We are leaving early Sunday morning. I can stay here Saturday night, if this helps."

Storing the glasses in the upper cabinet, Miguel insisted. "No … I'll be back right after the game tomorrow night. You'll be better rested for the drive if you sleep in your own bed."

A smile took hold, as Miguel envisioned game night … and those sparkling green eyes.

Lily scraped the syrupy glue from the veneer of the round table. The first week of classes had been satisfying but exhausting. Ribbons of construction paper, kaleidoscopic feathers, and self-adhesive foam shapes littered the mask-building station. The delighted teacher giggled as she recalled Aitor's presentation of Neptune, the human-robot-superhero who swallows his enemies and Blanca's Strawberry, the 700-year-old fairy who whips up pink fires. *An almost ideal day.*

"Claudia was able to talk to Mr. Losa when she supervised the pick-up of the students." Still wrapped in his red cape, Fergus flew in. "Mr. Losa told her that he has been divorced from Amaya's mother for some time now."

Lily clustered the scissors into the tin canister. "Amaya was feeling better at dismissal, but going into the weekend, I wanted her dad to be aware of what happened."

"Was she upset most of the day?" Straddling the chair, Fergus reclined.

Lily shook her head, heaving her leg onto the table. "This first week at camp, she has been pretty shy, but she volunteered to be the first to present her superhero to the class today."

"Aye. In the courtyard, I've seen her skipping rope—alone. Something's not right." Fergus's ginger eyebrows drew together.

Picking a worksheet from her desk, Lily scanned the paper. "She described her superhero Ama as a smart and funny thirty-seven-year-old with long, dark brown hair. Ama is brave but lives on another planet, sending helpful messages to kids through a magical laser. She started to cry when she told the class she wanted Ama to come back to Earth."

"Sounds like she misses her mam."

Pursing her lips, Lily suspected the circumstances were more complicated. "I'll keep a close eye on her, Fergus."

Tearing the bottom of the baguette, Miguel capped the piece with a slice of Roncal cheese, relieved that the weekend had arrived. Vacating his flat in the city and relocating to his mother's home had brought few hardships, except for the reunion with his childhood single bed. Gazing at the tired white kitchen cabinets brought familiarity and calm. As a teenager, Miguel would outline the shape of the cabinet doors in his mind, while his mother interrogated him about his late-night stunts. The kitchen table, swathed in a vinyl grey-quilted tablecloth, had witnessed their lives.

"She was very upset this afternoon, Miguel." His mother's knee bounced in a quick rhythm. Her visit with Isabel had shaken her.

Purging an olive pit from his mouth, his chest tingled. "I don't understand, Mamá. The meeting with Dr. Ortiz went well."

"Yes. Her recovery in the last few months has been steady." Scooping the last tomato slice, Miguel's mother gripped the fork firmly. "She has been able to relearn physical functions. He even said walking, with an aid, might be possible in the future."

"She's been having severe pain because of the herniated discs." Miguel mulled over his mother's distress. Isabel's depression had deepened but he kept this detail from her.

Lips mashing, Miguel ironed out a solution. "I'll spend the evening there with her, before going back to the B&B."

Tipping her head forward and sealing her heavy eyes, Miguel's mother pulled in his hand. "But don't you have plans with Antonio to watch the game?"

"Don't worry. I'll call him … I'll watch the game with Isa." Squeezing out a smile, Miguel collected the plates from the kitchen table. His mother's face softened as disappointment drizzled over his last bite of dinner.

"Slow down, I called Antonio. He's aware we are a tad late." Pausing to touch up her lipstick, Jade drifted like a visitor to an art gallery.

"A tad? The second half of the game has already started." Lily tried to walk faster, but Jade's platform sandals slowed them down.

A group of teenagers, sporting their team's jersey, blew out of a nearby restaurant. Lily moved forward and pointed at the red shirt worn by the lanky young man. "¿Cómo van?"

"Muy mal." This explained the strange calm of the streets, signalling a possible loss for the Spanish squad.

"Don't profess to be captivated by the game." Winking, Jade hurled her arm around Lily's neck.

Lily's chin dipped as Jade freed the grip. "I *am* interested in the game … and maybe other things, too." Lily sheepishly peered away.

"I find Miguel much too serious! But he *is* a hottie …"

Agreed. Glancing at the shop windows, Lily remembered their chance meeting outside of school.

Fending off the spotlight, Lily promptly changed the subject. "How are things with Fergus?"

Running her polished fingers through her golden hair, Jade tilted her head back. "Exhilarating! That man is *wild* in bed."

Lily craved Jade's confidence. An unrestrained laugh escaped her. "Wow! You have fulfilled your teenage fantasy. Fergus is not ignoring you now!"

"He's stopping over at La Perla for a nightcap." Looping her arm through Lily's, Jade was glowing. "Make sure you have your *own* plans this evening, sweetheart."

Nearing the Bodegón, the quivering in Lily's stomach mingled with promise.

With twelve minutes left, the ominous cloud of a scoreless match hovered. The packed bar held its breath. Stale, hot air clung to Lily's skin, as they coiled through the uneasy spectators.

Whispering behind Jade's ear, Lily's words were very direct. "We must *watch* the last few minutes and not talk, okay? It's a quarterfinal game—if they lose, they are eliminated."

Yanking out the stools, the friends sat between Antonio and the bar owner. "So pleased you made it!"

Riveted by the screen, Antonio quickly hugged them. "You didn't bring your boyfriend, Jade?"

Flapping her eyelashes, Jade's smug expression could not be contained. "You had your chance, darling!"

Lily discreetly combed the room. *Where is Miguel?* Studying her confused face, Antonio delivered unwelcome news. "Miguel isn't coming tonight. I'm sorry. He is with his sister … can I explain later?"

"Of course." Lily knew that her sunny voice would not deceive Jade.

Getting up, the bar owner's hand brushed Lily's drooping shoulder. "What can I get for you, ladies?"

Jade ordered as Lily unscrambled the muddle in her mind. "Two cañas and the potato-onion-omelette thingy we had last time."

Clarifying Jade's instructions, Lily interjected. "Tortilla, por favor."

"Muy bien." Flashing a genuine smile, Dani swung opposite the counter, as the eruption broke out.

"¡Gol!" Set ablaze from their seats like firecrackers, the bar patrons blasted their joy. The cheers in the Bodegón deafened the televised roar of the vuvuzela horns in the Johannesburg stadium. Tears fogged Antonio's glasses, as he squeezed Lily's hand. "You brought us luck!"

Jade looked puzzled. "Spain is wearing navy, not red? They should really keep it consistent." Lily light-heartedly shook her head, as she soaked up the replay of Villa's momentous goal.

To crown the occasion, their beer and food slid onto the table. Euphoric supporters blitzed the street, rejoicing in their team's promotion to the semi-final match against Germany. "Dani, otra cerveza." Antonio planted his fist on his chest as his red cheeks flamed. "This victory is historic for us."

Holding her beer, Lily patted Antonio's arm. "Congratulations! I consider myself very fortunate to be here in Spain during this World Cup." Antonio radiated, waving his arms overhead.

Jade curtly rolled her eyes at Lily. "Yes, congratulations … *rah, rah, rah* … Now, I believe you owe us an explanation, Antonio?"

Antonio smirked. "Jade doesn't love football. This is clear." Prompting a serious face, Antonio cleared his throat. "Miguel's sister, Isabel, is in the hospital."

Setting her hand to her mouth, Lily's features darkened.

"This really isn't my story to tell, but I can say that she had a very serious accident in January and has been there for months."

The high of the match disappeared in a flash. "I'm sorry to hear this." The appetizing last bit of tortilla sat numb on Lily's plate.

"Isabel is supposed to come home soon, which is very good news, but today was a bad day for her. Miguel thought it best to visit with her tonight." Antonio's consoling eyes peered at Lily.

"He is certainly a superior brother to mine. Logan would be incapable of shuffling his evening plans to keep *me* company, even on my deathbed!" As Jade sneered, Lily bobbed her head in agreement.

"Miguel does want to spend Thursday, the eighth of July with you, unless you already have plans. He is running the B&B on his own for most of next week." A carefree smile extended over Lily's lips.

"She has no plans!" Jade jumped in sooner than Lily could reply.

"Wonderful! He wants to meet you at seven a.m. by the kiosk at the Plaza del Castillo, which is close to your hotel."

Grimacing, Jade shook her head. "What a dreadful hour!" Lily paused. *My hotel?*

"It will be a long day of San Fermín activities, but a fantastic one, I hope. We can all meet in the evening at the fireworks." Appearing gratified with his coordination, Antonio guzzled the last suds.

Jade applauded like a child awaiting a parade. "I love fireworks!"

"If *I* could speak ..." Hilarity took over their corner of the bar, as Lily rapped her finger on the tabletop.

Her gleaming eyes snapped back. "Let Miguel know I'll be there at seven. Sharp."

CHAPTER EIGHT

The sweat rolled along his flaming cheek, as he lifted the bucket stuffed with cleaning supplies. The residual bouquet of lemon reassured Miguel that he had done a decent job. He preferred to undertake the laundry, dusting, and vacuuming—bathroom cleaning was gruelling for him. With the guesthouse completely full, the last four days had been overrun by domestic chores. Speedy Elena made housekeeping appear painless. *I miss her!* He was comfortable in the kitchen, so taking over Isabel's duties was effortless. Arrogance convinced him that tidying his flat in Pamplona equipped him for *this*. He'd been humbled. Rest would return tomorrow.

The Japanese students and the British couple were travellers on the Camino de Santiago, lodging for only one night at the B&B. Miguel would straighten their rooms later. Dashing downstairs, he flopped on the patio recliner for a quick rest.

While most of the Camino pilgrims are accommodated at inexpensive dormitories, his guests yearned for one night of pampering, including a comfortable bed and a private shower. Since the ninth century, thousands of pilgrims roamed this town, Puente La Reina, on their way to the far northwestern corner of Spain. The end point was the shrine of St. James, within the cathedral in Santiago de Compostela.

Isabel cherished these Camino visitors who kept her B&B open, even in the off-season. Miguel appreciated their rich conversations over the breakfast table. Waking twenty kilometres a day, these pilgrims had the time to reflect, to probe inward, to modify priorities, and to savour the virtues of living. Miguel respected the power of this ancient journey and imagined it might comfort his own headspace.

With the camp closed for the San Fermín festival, Alegría Language School was converted into a sports bar, complete with drinks, snacks, flags, and lots of cheering. The staff was fully prepared for the semi-final match. Lily delighted in the camaraderie and the sangría, as she watched her first complete World Cup match. She knew she would miss her colleagues this coming holiday week.

After the match, Fergus and Lily spilled out of the academy, swept up in the dancing crowds, en route to meet Jade. They wore all white, except for the red neck scarves and waist sashes—the "uniform" of the San Fermín fiestas. The atmosphere throughout Pamplona was electric that night, as July seventh was also the city's patron saint's day.

"Puyol is a beast!" Impressed by the Spanish player's header, Fergus drummed his rugged hand on Lily's arm. With a victory over Germany, the feeling of euphoria took over the city. "San Fermín is always a tremendous street party, lass, but this scale of merriment is unparalleled!"

Hollering over the music, Lily's voice was hoarse. "Every aspect of this trip has been *unparalleled* for me! I feel so at home here. I guess I have Jade to thank for pushing me to come." Lily clutched Fergus's burly arm, as he navigated the ancient roadway.

"Aye. She won't let you forget it, either!" Chuckling, Lily grinned broadly. "I'm happy for you, sweetheart. I know it's been a challenging year." Fergus gave her shoulder a generous squeeze.

"I think I desperately needed a vacation or Pamplona truly agrees with me!" Without notice, Lily's white T-shirt and pants absorbed the red wine downpour from the cup of a plastered young man.

Howling, Fergus sprang back. "Well, you've been baptized now, Lil!"

Planting themselves on the broad sectional of the common room, the friends set their wine glasses on the mahogany coffee table. The aroma of fried txistorra sausage strayed from the kitchen. Miguel released a profound breath. He had weathered Elena's absence and would now attend to the semi-final match of the World Cup. Miguel sunk into the sofa.

"Thanks for coming to Puente to watch the game." Restless, Antonio fidgeted with the zipper of the decorative pillow on his lap.

Muting the pre-game banter from the television, Miguel pressed his friend. "Is everything ok? You seem out of sorts."

Staring at the sloped ceiling beams, Antonio's hands blanketed his face. "I'm nervous to tell you about an arrangement I made."

Bouncing from his reclined position, Miguel recalled the last *arrangement* his friend had made: escorting Antonio's folksy cousin to a family wedding, shortly after his sister's accident, was claimed to be therapeutic—it was actually a very long night of misery. "What did you do?"

Dodging eye contact, Antonio focussed on the hand-knit chambray pillow. "You remember the other night when you couldn't come to the game at the Bodegón?"

"Yes—when I went to the hospital?" Miguel's eyes harpooned Antonio's temple.

Cagily, Antonio boosted his head. "Lily looked genuinely upset about Isabel … and about you not joining us."

Surprisingly moved, Miguel guarded his reaction. "And …?"

At record speed, Antonio burst out. "I told Lily you would spend the whole day with her tomorrow." Plunging back into the sofa, Miguel shook his head. "I *know* you like her, and she would love to spend the day with you. Where's the harm in making this happen?"

Slumped, Miguel kept silent. His relationship with Susana had left a durable knot of scars. "Didn't *you* invite her to the game last Saturday night?" Antonio sloped in, seeking Miguel's reaction.

"Yes ... I did it impulsively when I saw her on the street. When it didn't work out, I *knew* it was a sign to leave it alone. It's easier this way." Miguel also understood his powerlessness to remove Lily from his thoughts.

Filling his wine glass, Antonio remained calm. "It's one day, Miguel. I haven't signed you up for marriage classes!"

With a smile reclaiming his face, Miguel snagged the remote control and restored the volume. "So, exactly *what* am I doing tomorrow?"

Waving like a princess, Jade surfaced. "Finally! I presumed I had misinterpreted the meeting spot: White Horse. I tried to call you, Fergus."

Planting a confident kiss, Fergus momentarily sealed Jade's lips.

"I forgot my mobile at school, love." Positioning his arms around the two women, Fergus marshalled them to the rim of the defensive wall. "The Caballo Blanco is my favourite nook in the city." Overtop the sixteenth century El Redín bastion, the panorama of the city neighbourhoods below, and the surrounding mountains, was dazzling. Lily scanned the fortifications defending Pamplona's historic core, as she hoped to dismantle her own fortress.

Leaning her head on Fergus's shoulder, Jade rattled the silence. "The Mesón's terrace was utterly full. My charm was futile in persuading the host to seat us."

"Your charm has *me* spellbound, darling."

Jade's eyes glistened, as she lobbed him an air kiss. Eager that this fling would evolve into an enduring bond, Lily understood how ideal Fergus was for Jade. She shamefully juggled this joy with her own pangs of envy. Jade easily achieved anything she desired. Lily had never been brushed by this feeling.

Adjusting her sticky T-shirt, Lily pushed aside the fog in her head. "I think I've had my fill of vino today. I'm even wearing it!"

Fergus flashed her a mischievous grin.

"Let's unwind at my hotel. I can't bear these packed streets." Jade and Fergus slid off the wall, shaking out their legs.

Speaking in a bubbly pitch, Lily flung her arms out wide, hugging the couple. "I think I'm going to head back to the pensión. I have an early morning."

"The big date! So, we'll rendezvous at the fireworks, after? I'm meeting you first, Fergus, following the spa, at Café Iruña."

Lily's face lit, as she fidgeted with the strap of her purse. "Sure."

Quizzing Jade with the coolness of an older brother, Fergus's eyebrows curled. "Do we like this Miguel?"

Jade grabbed Lily's hand. "We do."

CHAPTER NINE

Parked on a copper bench opposite the kiosk, Miguel soaked in the morning rays jetting through the Plaza del Castillo. The distant sound of the municipal brass band music known as Las Dianas, woke up the ancient roads below. Lining the square, dormant terraces were cleansed, and groomed, anticipating the crush of visitors. Dishevelled partygoers crossed the square, entering the barricaded streets to run with the bulls, while others slumbered in the surrounding gardens.

Miguel scanned the square for Lily. His initial resistance to Antonio's *arrangement* had vanished, replaced by eagerness. The early birds, seniors, and young families journeyed about wearing their spotless white shirts and pants; red scarves adding a splash of colour. Strolling from the opposite direction, Miguel spotted the wagging caramel ponytail and wispy bangs that framed her oval face. Waving, Lily jogged over to the bench. As she approached, the perfume of lavender soap honeyed the air.

"Good morning, Miguel." He stood to kiss her, noticing the freckles dotting her rosy cheeks.

"Buenos días. I thought you were walking over from your hotel?" Miguel signalled the right corner of the square. Lily sprung one bent knee on the bench, facing him.

"Hotel? Oh … La Perla. No, Jade is staying there. I'm at a pensión on Mayor Street."

"I'm sorry. I guess I misunderstood." Miguel pushed away faint embarrassment at his knee-jerk assumptions about Lily.

Lily's moss green eyes shone in the morning light, as she tilted her head. "How is your sister doing?"

"A bit better. She is supposed to be coming home, soon." Knots settled in his belly; he recognized Lily's genuine kindness even as he steered the conversation onto safer territory. "I hope you are well rested for a busy day of fun! We need to make your father's trip memorable."

Lily's eyes enlarged as she raised a thumbs up. "The Running of the Bulls is our first stop, I assume?"

Adjusting the red scarf or pañuelo around her neck, Miguel admired the multiple silver hoops, fitted snuggly to her petite ear lobes. Catching himself, he pulled his gaze.

"Yes, the encierro starts at eight, but we will need to find a spot on the street to see it."

Plucking a key card out of her crossbody purse, Lily offered a solution. "Let's watch it from Jade's balcony over Estafeta. She can join us—if she's up."

"Are you sure? Will she mind?" A strange nervousness crawled into his stomach.

Smiling broadly, Lily giggled as she twisted the wine-stained laces of her Converse. "Not at all! She begged me to stay with her for this trip, but I'm stubborn about paying my own way."

"It's a historic hotel. Are you sure you made the right decision?"

Lily leaned her head towards her shoulder, as tresses of hair floated along her temples. "Maybe not ... I do find it hard to accept help." Her bright eyes darkened.

Rubbing the back of his neck, Miguel confessed, "That takes strength, Lily. I would not have survived these last few months without the help of my family and friends."

"Strength or necessity? I grew up with no family except my father. I've always had to take care of myself."

Shuffling his feet, Miguel reflected on Lily piloting her life, with little family support. His admiration for her grew. Miguel forced his growing nerves to take a back seat. *This moment would be for Lily.* He squeezed her hand and hiked her off the bench. "I believe a balcony is waiting for us!"

Skulking through the living room, Lily and Miguel sidestepped the swarm of pillows cluttering the wood floor of Jade's studio. It was visible through the glass wall that her friends were in a deep sleep. Fergus's snoring pierced the calm of the hotel suite.

Lily gently turned the lock on the chalk-white balcony door. As she filed out behind Miguel, Lily was struck by the vitality of the street. Surrounded by clusters of people nestled on every balcony, Lily looked down and imagined the nerves fluttering in the bellies of the runners.

"This is the best place to see the encierro." Grinning broadly, Miguel's chocolate eyes journeyed through Estafeta. Masked by looking sideways, Lily took note of his sharp cheekbones, broad nose, and full lips. His usual serious face was transformed when he smiled.

"Have you done this run?"

"Yes ... many times." Drawing her closer to the corner of the balcony, Miguel pointed. His lemony cologne shrouded Lily's attention. "Antonio and I would run the first stretch at the slope of Santo Domingo. Estafeta is the last part of the run."

Lifting her head, Lily recalled *Guide to Northern Spain*. "This tradition dates back to the thirteenth century!" Miguel nodded. *Stop sounding like a teacher, Lily.*

Placing her hand on his shoulder, Lily leaned in, as the street chatter amplified. She saw scores of runners roaming the freshly washed road. Momentarily brushing her lips to his ear, Miguel's breathing deepened as he explained what was about to transpire. "At eight sharp the first rocket is set off to announce the opening of the bullpens. The six trained steers are the first out. Then, the second rocket is launched, when the six fighting bulls have left the pens."

Curving to face him, Lily stepped back. "I remember my father boasting that the goal of the runner is to sprint in front of the bull's horns. This sounds terrifying to me." Sweeping a strand of hair from Lily's cheek, Miguel shook his head. His touch made her stomach gently flip.

"With so many runners, few can do this. Most just avoid getting trampled."

The blast of the first rocket sprung Lily against the doorway. Miguel laughed as he guided her to stand in front of him. Securely encased by his body and the railing, every nerve inside of her came alive.

Like a choreographed dance, the multitude below slowly moved forward, steadily increasing the tempo. The pace suddenly erupted into a panicked rush, as the flow of runners split down the middle, allowing the steers and bulls to stampede through the red and white sea. The rattle of the cowbells mixed with the clapping, whistling, and cheering from the spectators. Lily's skin tingled.

"Look. One of the bulls has turned back. This is very dangerous." Perching his chin on her shoulder, his breath brushed the side of her face. Her eyes were glued to the action below, while her mind wandered. Miguel abruptly stepped back, just as the bull was safely redirected.

The spectacle was as thrilling as the company, but Lily was strangely overcome by sadness. Flustered by her emerging tears, she drew a tissue from her purse, hoping Miguel had not noticed.

Stepping beside her, his sable eyebrows furrowed. "Are you ok?"

"Yes. It's silly." Forcing a smile, while swallowing to clear the lump in her throat, Lily slipped back into the studio to compose herself. Miguel followed.

Tears gushed as she whispered her muddled state. "I wish my father had been able to see this … I miss him so much." Miguel tightly wrapped his golden arms around her slender frame. Lily's head cocooned in the curve of his shoulder, as the beat of his heart pulsing hushed the sorrow. Calm slowly washed over her. They stood in silence, oblivious to time.

Lost in the moment, Lily impulsively elevated her head and anchored her tear-stained lips onto his mouth. The prickly tension she permanently housed, melted away for a brief second, replaced by a haze of pleasure. Her heart quivered as she floated off.

What am I doing? Her brain took command releasing the kiss and ending the intimate moment. Her eyes fixated on the floor. "I'm sorry, Miguel."

He slid his smooth palm beneath her chin, nervously lifting her face. His protective hands were clumsy as they cupped her two burning cheeks. Miguel's dizzy brown eyes burned into hers with a blend of longing and compassion. "I'm … I'm *not* sorry, Lily."

The tender kiss halted her breath. Lily's arms encircled his neck, bracing her to his toned body. Her hands played in his wavy hair, as their lips sparked.

"Good morning!" Like the jolting end of an exhilarating rollercoaster ride, Miguel and Lily hesitantly disconnected and turned. Arms crossed along her white robe, Jade's smirk fused with her approving eyes.

Miguel took Lily's hand and made a beeline towards the door, rattling the vase of roses as they bumped into the coffee table. "Thank you for the use of the balcony, Jade. See you at the fireworks tonight!" Lily waved as she was swept through the doorway.

CHAPTER TEN

The line outside the coffeehouse on Mañueta Street was not terribly long, considering the legendary status of their chocolate con churros. Miguel's brisk escape from La Perla had secured a favourable spot in line for this classic San Fermín breakfast. "The wait is worth it."

Still cradling his hand, Lily closed her eyes and inhaled deeply. "I'm savouring the sweet aroma in the air. It's making me hungry." Nodding in agreement, Miguel smiled. His craving went beyond the strips of fried sugary dough. "My colleague Mateo, from school, told me about this place. The same family has been running the business for generations."

Miguel nodded as he watched the server cut the jumbo donut spiral into smaller portions and generously sprinkle the sugar. He passed the warm package of churros to Lily and carried out the two cups of hot chocolate, thick as pudding.

"This is divine!" Lily zealously dipped the morsel into the chocolate.

It had been a few years since Miguel last visited this churrería. His ex, Susana, was always on some diet, restricting decadent breakfasts. Lily seemed open to trying anything.

Wiping the extra chocolate from his mouth, Miguel offered Lily more. "I know you are a teacher, but did you say you work *here*, at a school?"

"Yes. I'm teaching English at a summer day camp. It's helping me to finance this trip."

Embarrassed at having dismissed her as a rich tourist, Miguel stared at her brilliant green eyes.

"My colleagues are wonderful, and the kids are great. We have a lot of fun together. It seems dishonest to take a paycheque."

Scouring the last bit of sugar from the corner of the white package, Miguel directed them towards a quiet street. "What's the name of the school?"

"Alegría Language School." His eyes widened in recognition. "You know it?" Lily's voice soared with interest.

"My niece attends this program. The day I ran into you, I had dropped her off." It was crystal clear to him now. Lily had said she was late for work, but he was too absorbed in their chance meeting to link the puzzle pieces.

"What's her name?" Lily dashed over to the trash can as Miguel responded.

"Amaya."

Her delicate face hardened. "Amaya Losa?"

"Yes. Well, her full name is Amaya Losa Martínez." Miguel's face radiated. "*You* know Amaya?" Energized, his stride quickened.

"Yes. She is in my class this session. Amaya is a very sweet girl." Lily looked down at the cobblestones of Redín Street.

"How is she in class? She has been having a very difficult time since Isabel's accident." Slowing, Miguel pointed to a grassy area by the fortified walls of the Caballo Blanco. They sat in a shady spot on the lawn, leaning against the stone barricade.

Lily's face had not softened. "Amaya is Isabel's daughter? … makes sense."

"What do you mean?" Miguel rubbed his forearms, sensing a weightiness between them. Lily shifted away from the wall to face him. She wrapped her arms around her shaky bent knees.

"Amaya is struggling. She isolates herself from the other kids and seems very sad most days." Lily's kind eyes tried to cushion the impact, but Miguel felt gutted. He reached for his cigarette pack.

Exhaling deeply, Miguel's serious face resurfaced. "This breaks my heart. I thought the day camp would be an enjoyable distraction for her."

"Has Amaya seen her mom since the accident? I know they talk on the phone every day, but does she visit?" Lily's tone was sympathetic, but Miguel felt uncomfortable with her questions.

Narrowing his eyes on the pack in his hand, he curtly responded. "No. It's complicated. Isabel prefers her daughter not to visit her in person for now." The intense guilt over his sister's predicament was gurgling deep inside.

Lily inched closer, placing her hand on Miguel's knee. "I cannot imagine how challenging this is on your sister, but I think her decision is hurting Amaya a great deal. She is a child who is feeling abandoned. I know the feeling well. She needs physical contact with her mother, Miguel." A flood of dread engulfed him, as her words bounced off the stone wall. *Why is she judging my family? I'm doing my best.*

Avoiding eye contact, Miguel stared at the Marlboros, as his face reddened. "You don't know the whole story, Lily. My sister is trying to *survive*—she is not 'abandoning' her daughter! How can you see Amaya for only a few hours a day and think you have all the solutions?"

Pulling her hand from his knee, Lily spoke slowly with a quiver in her voice. "I'm sorry if I'm upsetting you, Miguel. I don't pretend to have the answers, but I want you to think about Amaya. She is a smart kid who can understand her mom's new reality and who wants to help her."

Miguel sprang to his feet, hoisted by shame. Dusting off his white pants, he looked into Lily's watery eyes. "Don't tell me I'm not thinking about my family!"

Lily vaulted herself to stand. "That isn't what I meant!"

"Today was a mistake. I should have never allowed Antonio to talk me into it." He could see how his words crushed Lily. Her mouth dropped open, disbelief settling on her tense face. "I need to go." Overwhelmed with the complexity of the moment, he turned and vanished into the crowd.

The large dining room sparkled with gilded light, transporting visitors back to the nineteenth century. Large, finely polished mirrors and arabesque pillars rose to the decorated mouldings and chandeliers of the ceiling. As Lily recounted the day's events to Jade and Fergus, the splendour of the Café Iruña brightened her mood but could not salvage her devoured nails.

She had squandered the day alone, fueled by an ugly soup of anger, frustration, and confusion. Lily deconstructed their conversation and replayed the same scene: Miguel walking away. That familiar feeling of abandonment enveloped her. How could such a beautiful morning collapse so rapidly?

"Maybe I pushed too hard? His family is going through a great deal." Crossing her arms over her stomach, Lily's patatas bravas sat untouched.

Jade's spa calm was replaced by sisterly concern. "That doesn't excuse his insensitive comments." The flute of bubbly Cava rested by Jade's pristine manicured hand. Lily knew she was right.

Reaching over to pick at Lily's spicy potatoes, Fergus interjected. "It sounds like Miguel has too much on his plate. Best to keep your distance, love. After the San Fermín holiday, I will take you off yard duty in the morning, so you don't run into him when he drops off Amaya." Fergus gently placed his hand on Lily's shoulder, as she fixated on the black and white tiled floor.

"I suppose." Her father's piece of advice flashed. *Stop moping, Lily Bear. Pick yourself up and move on.* Breathing profoundly to cleanse the day away, she steadied herself and tried to hold on to the incredible experience at Jade's studio—before everything unravelled.

"Are you certain about the fireworks?" Jade's skeptical smile highlighted her concern.

Gulping her Cava, Lily questioned whether she would even be happy to see Miguel or whether he would bother to show up with Antonio. Either way, she was determined to make her last three weeks in Spain extraordinary. Lily owed this to her Pops. It had been a mistake to believe that a unique bond existed with this stranger.

A calm smile radiated across her face, as she leaned in. "I'm looking forward to it."

Rapping gently on his bedroom door, Miguel's mother called out. "Are you hungry?"

After leaving Lily that morning, he had spent most of his prized vacation day in bed, ruminating, and sleeping. His tense body had rested, but his thoughts remained tangled. Embarrassed by his response to Lily's honest questions, Miguel knew he had overreacted. He owed her a mammoth apology.

"Yes. Thanks, Mamá. I'll be right out." Flinging on his white T-shirt, he found a chocolate stain by the collar. His mind flooded with the image of Lily's chocolate-covered mouth, delighting in each bite of the churro.

Kissing his mother's cheek as he entered the kitchen, his stomach growled at the frying pan where a whole trout, stuffed with slices of jamón serrano, hissed. Filling the glasses with red wine, Miguel reached for the baguette on the counter. A bright bowl of cherries caught his eye. "Amaya's favourite! Is she staying over at her Tía Sara's place? I was hoping to take her to the fireworks tonight."

His mother beamed as she placed the salad on the table. "She loves being with her cousins, but don't worry, she is coming back soon."

Swallowing the first bite of his dinner, Miguel's rattled state needed his mother's advice. "Do you think Amaya should see Isabel at the hospital? Was it a mistake to keep her away?" His despairing eyes closed as he shook his head. "Should we have encouraged Isabel to change her mind?"

His mother's face was visibly alarmed by the onslaught of questions. "Miguel, where is this all coming from?"

"One of Amaya's camp teachers, who I know, suggested she should see her mother. She thought not seeing Isabel was hurting her." Lily had forced him into thorny territory.

Passing him the salad bowl, Miguel's mother paused before speaking. "I agree with the teacher. I guess she doesn't realize how stubborn my children are!" Cracking the tension, they both laughed. "Perhaps we could do more to convince Isabel. I believe this will be good for both of them."

Taking a swig of wine, Miguel nodded. Comforted by his mother's words, he quietly exhaled. "Maybe we can talk to her about it on Saturday when we visit." A spark of guilt flashed, acknowledging that he had overlooked Amaya's feelings in his concern over Isabel's needs.

His mother's face remained agitated. "What's wrong, Mamá?"

"I've decided about Casa Emi. You are not going to like what you hear."

Miguel held his breath.

"I am going to sell the B&B." His fork nosedived, clinking the ceramic plate. "We can then pay all of Isabel's bills and you can go back to running the café and living on your own."

Nervous energy charged in all directions. The tension in his chest quickly returned. "But the house has been in the family for so long, Mamá."

"*People* make a home, not bricks, and stone, Miguel."

"And what about Isabel? The B&B was her dream!"

Sighing, Miguel's mother took his hand. "I have spent many sleepless nights thinking about this very point, and I even consulted with Dr. Ortiz. The B&B *could* be healing for Isabel, or it might frustrate her ... given that her role at the inn will change. Her doctor thought having her work just a few hours at Café Miisa, with you, would be a smoother transition." Gathering the dishes from the table, Miguel placed them into the empty sink.

Walloped by his mother's decision, Miguel's head reeled. "I don't know what to say."

His mother rubbed his back and directed him to sit.

"You don't have to say anything about this." She kissed the top of his head and circled towards the kitchen sink.

Miguel needed a plan to stop the sale of the B&B—but that would have to wait. Right now, reuniting Amaya and his sister needed his full attention.

CHAPTER ELEVEN

The Citadel Park was overflowing with families, friends, and couples sharing blankets on the lush green lawn. Lily popped on her white sweatshirt and arranged her red pañuelo, as Jade ushered them through the patchwork. Jade spotted Miguel sitting with Antonio and Amaya, waiting for the fireworks to begin. She gripped Lily's hand forcefully.

"I'm fine, Jade." A nervous pang emerged in her stomach; nothing she couldn't handle. But why did he need to look so good tonight? His olive complexion contrasted divinely with his white cotton shirt and black hair.

The introductions were a blur. Lily embraced the quiet child and Amaya followed her to the blanket Fergus had laid out. He had instinctively positioned himself in the middle, with Jade beside Antonio, and Lily farthest away.

"Are you okay, lass?"

Lily gave a thumbs up as she reclined on the ground, combing the smooth cool grass with her hand. Amaya dropped her purple mini backpack and lay beside Lily, snuggling a bit closer to her teacher. Waiting for the show to begin, Lily rested her eyes, tuning into her friends' chatter, disappointed that she yearned to hear Miguel's voice.

Lily's body loosened, as the pyrotechnical show commenced. The fire, light, and sound display was a magnificent spectacle. With her attention hooked on the twinkling bursts and whirls of colour above, Lily's edginess eased. Following the coiling and zooming illuminations, the half hour swiftly flew.

"Wasn't that exciting Amaya?" The girl sat up and nodded as she slipped a notebook and a crayon pack from her bag. As the child set up her art studio on the corner of the blanket, Lily glanced over at Jade and Fergus. They were still lying in a deep embrace staring at the night sky, illuminated by a brilliant moon. Why couldn't she have that?

Lily took in his citrus scent even before she saw him. Miguel settled in beside Amaya, gently kissing her forehead and stroking her hair as the girl looked down to select the perfect crayon. "Did you enjoy the fireworks?"

"Sí, mucho." Miguel handed her a small bag of popcorn. "That's a perfect colour for the mermaid's tail, Amaya." The girl looked up and broke a smile. Lily wrapped her arms around her knees and looked straight ahead pretending not to have been stirred by Miguel's tenderness towards his niece.

"Lily, can we talk?" While most of the spectators stood to leave the park, Lily turned to face him as he moved closer to her corner of the blanket. Her pulse quickened. She remained silent, as anger and compassion wrestled for her attention.

Lily avoided his eyes as she twisted the corner of the navy blanket. He spoke in a hushed jittery voice. "Lily, I don't know what happened this morning. I was out of line." As he reached for his ratty cigarette pack, Lily noticed a small wrist tattoo usually hidden by his bracelets. The name *J. Mari*, in black ink, stared at her. *How could I fall for someone I know so little about?*

Looking up, Lily pierced his gaze. "Is this how *you* feel, or did Antonio convince you to say this?" She released some of her anger.

Taken aback, Miguel's eyes widened acknowledging Lily's feistiness. "Fair. My comment about Antonio was unkind. Truthfully, the date idea was not mine, but I was very appreciative he arranged it."

"You have a strange way of showing it!" Looking over her shoulder, Amaya was busy with her drawing. Lily needed to keep her volume down.

Furrowing his forehead, Miguel moved closer filling the space between them with his citrus scent. His whisper grew louder. "Listen, I think we can agree we *both* went too far."

"*Both?* Are you serious Miguel?" Her chest was about to explode.

"Well, yes ... maybe you overstepped with your comments."

"Well, maybe *you* can't handle honest questions." Red-faced, Miguel was about to respond when his niece called him.

Waving her completed drawing of a mermaid swimming beneath a night sky bursting with fireworks, Amaya instantly lowered the heat. "Look, Tío!"

"Beautiful work, Amaya." He held the drawing, studying every detail. His steely face returned. "I think I need to take this talented artist home." Slowly rising, Lily stretched her legs. Amaya rammed her crayons into the pack and Miguel took out his car keys. The tension congealed around them.

"Thanks for watching the fireworks with me, Amaya." The child approached and hugged Lily's waist.

"For you." Amaya proudly handed Lily her drawing. Lily held it to her chest.

This was the highlight of her evening. "Gracias, sweetheart."

"Good night, Lily." Miguel leaned in for the traditional farewell kiss as Lily carefully dodged his lips.

"Goodbye Miguel."

The aroma of the pastries he carried blended harmoniously with the coffee Elena brewed. Miguel set down the box, throwing his keys and cigarettes into the top drawer of the chef's desk. As he reached for his apron, the promise of a new day emerged, serenaded by the song of warblers and larks outside the kitchen window. Ruining any chance with Lily yesterday had crumbled his heart—why did their tempers flare so quickly? Now, he would focus on his family and try to forget her. Miguel thought about taking Amaya to the Menudas Fiestas tomorrow. She would enjoy the bouncy castle, puppet shows, and especially the handicrafts.

"Buenos días, Elena. How is your Friday going?"

She rocked her head as she marched towards him. "You are in trouble, my friend." Elena's hair was wet as she thrust her fuchsia toiletries bag into her tote on the harvest table. "Javier installed the ramps. He said *you* told him to go ahead and finish the job."

Miguel's devious smile appeared to annoy Elena. "Yes. They turned out very well."

"But your mother—"

"I know what my mother said, but the ramps make sense whether we keep the inn or sell it. Javier is coming back next week to install the handrails in the bathroom."

Looping the stuffed bag over her shoulder, Elena grimaced. "She didn't want the added expense, Miguel."

He placed his calm hand on Elena's shoulder and spoke with certainty. "It's not too costly, and these changes will help Isabel adjust."

Her stern face unsettled him. "Miguel, you need to accept that she is putting this house up for sale."

Like a drowning man reaching for a life buoy, Miguel would not surrender. "We have to find another solution."

"I hope you find it fast. A real estate agent is coming on Monday." Elena kissed his cheek as she crossed to the door. "See you tomorrow morning."

Lifting the receiver, Miguel called Amaya to discuss their plans for Saturday.

With all her white shorts and pants demanding a wash, Lily opted for her short floral skirt. After a turbulent night, extra sleep was preferred over a visit to the laundromat. Still maintaining the San Fermín look with her white tank top and pañuelo, Lily entered Arco Íris.

The door chime resembled the score of a Harry Potter film. It was an enchanting way to float into this oasis. The brightly coloured shelves, spinners flaunting picture books, and the splashy posters skirting the top edge of the walls, coordinated well with the mini-armchairs and bean bag seats. Browsing for books would be a delight, while she waited for Jade to review the new website with Antonio. Her anger towards Miguel remained … and so did the attraction. Lily craved peace and clarity. She hoped Arco Íris would do the trick.

"Buenos días." Lily ambled towards the back of the bookstore. Jade and Antonio were hidden behind the desktop monitor. Antonio's associate was unpacking a box behind them. "How's it looking?"

"I'm very happy with it so far." Antonio stood to say hello. Jade waved and blew Lily a kiss. "How are you doing?" Antonio's eyes analyzed her face.

Lily replied, dodging the real question. "I'm in heaven. Your shop is amazing!"

He rested his hand on Lily's shoulder and drew closer. "I'm sorry I was dishonest with you about the date with Miguel. I haven't seen him so happy with anyone since the accident. I got carried away." *Now that's an apology.*

Lily's stomach tightened. "Don't worry. Your heart was in the right place."

Jade's head popped up. "Antonio, could you please bring your heart over *here*? We need to finish." They both rolled their eyes, accustomed to Jade's impatience.

Lily journeyed to the back of the shop where the glittering orange sign, LIBROS EN INGLÉS, twirled above the bookshelves. She could always use more resources for her Reading Corner. "Hello, I don't believe we have formally met. My name is Lucas." The tall blonde wiped his dusty palm on his jeans before reaching out to firmly shake Lily's hand. His hazel eyes studied her face. "You are Lily, correct?"

His hand loitered. "Yes. Nice to meet you."

"I feel like I know you, from eavesdropping on Jade and Antonio." Unapologetic, as he chuckled, Lucas drew out magazines from a box. He moved with the confidence of a person who values his attractiveness.

"Oh, no! I hope they painted a favourable picture!" Lily tried to keep the mood light, as she thumbed through *Matilda*.

Lucas stopped, his eyes scaling her body until they reached Lily's blushing face. "A very enticing picture, I would say."

Regaining her focus, Lily put down the book. "Well, that's not fair. I know nothing about you."

"Ok. Let's change this. I'm about to go on a short break. Would you join me for a coffee?" His flirtations comforted her wounded pride and gave her a break from thinking about Miguel.

"Why not?" His firm hand rested on her back as he directed Lily to the door.

Jade stood up as they passed, looking bewildered. "I'm almost done, Lil. Be back soon."

The magical door chime ushered them out. "Is she always so demanding?" Lucas now had his arm around her as they approached the cute café at the end of the street. Lily wasn't entirely comfortable with this bold move, but it felt good to be noticed.

"That's just Jade. She is very direct but means well." Lucas rolled his eyes, not convinced.

The table by the front window was empty. Lucas brought two cafés con leche and dragged his chair over so that it was beside hers. Lucas's confidence was a bit much. She pulled her chair back.

"So ... things didn't work out with Miguelito?" He took his time licking the froth off his upper lip.

Feeling awkward and a bit shocked, Lily didn't know what to say. "I'd rather not talk about it."

"Of course ... I'm sorry, Lily. I totally understand. Miguel is incapable of appreciating a beautiful woman, like you." Lily didn't entirely agree but she was still upset, and it felt reassuring to have someone on her side.

"I don't know ... His personal life is overwhelming, but you must know this given your talent at eavesdropping." She flashed him a cheeky smile and gulped down the last drop of coffee.

Narrowing his eyes, Lucas's bright face took a serious turn. "We were once very close friends, actually ... Anyway, he has changed dramatically since his girlfriend was killed in a car accident last January."

A surge of dread numbed Lily's body. Miguel's wrist tattoo flashed. Of course, her name must be *J. Mari*. "This is horrible! Was that the same accident Isabel had? I thought she was alone." Lily's mind raced as she tried to make sense of these details.

"Yes. They were together in the car when it collided with a truck on the highway." She was speechless, as her shocked eyes welled. Lily's heart broke for this young woman who lost her life, for Isabel who intimately shared this tragedy, and for Miguel who was lost in grief. Why didn't *he* tell her about the loss of his girlfriend? She sat in silence for what resembled an eternity.

Lucas covered Lily's hand with his. "As you say in English, 'life goes on.' Isabel is doing better, which is great news."

Lily's jumbled head could put few words together. "Yes." Had she been too hard on Miguel? She forced a smile and exhaled slowly, hoping her scrambled thoughts would settle.

"I need to cheer you up." Brushing a hand through his golden hair, Lucas leaned towards her. "When do you return home?"

"In three weeks." Saying those words reminded Lily of the promise she had made to herself. These last three weeks needed to be drama-free and wonderful.

Lucas rubbed his hands together, his face beaming. "I would love to show you San Sebastian. The beaches are gorgeous, and the food is outstanding. We could be there in an hour and a bit."

Not ready for such an excursion with the handsome but overly assertive Lucas, Lily leaned back in her chair. "I'll let you know." If Miguel had asked, she would have no hesitation.

As they walked back to the bookstore, Lucas tried again. "Have you seen the parade of Giants and Big-Heads?"

"My students at Alegría told me about this. It's their favourite part of the Festival. I promised them I would check it out."

"Perfect—it's a date! I can meet you at nine, tomorrow morning. Where are you staying?" *Wow. Lucas was a determined one!* She considered her options. Jade was not an early bird while on vacation and she had promised her students she would go. Why not?

"I'm at Pensión Itxaro on Mayor street."

"I know it." Caressing her arm, he departed with the common two-cheek kiss. Not surprisingly, Lucas's goodbye included a slight brush of her lips.

CHAPTER TWELVE

Lily cleared the sweat from her forehead, as they navigated the Saturday morning crowd of onlookers, along the parade route. Lucas insisted on holding her hand, as they sandwiched their way to the front. He didn't get the hint when she dropped his clasp numerous times.

Charmed by the colossal papier-mâché kings and queens, Lily shimmied her way forward to take a picture. She could feel Lucas's breath on her back as she crouched for the perfect shot.

Her students at Alegría had urged her to see this spectacle, their favourite part of San Fermín. The kids enjoyed being chased by the half-horse, half-man Zaldíkos, and the Kilikis wielding their sponge batons. Lily was delighted by their recommendation but less thrilled with her clingy companion.

Four pairs of royal giants representing the continents of Europe, Africa, Asia, and the Americas waltzed with agility and elegance to the music of drums and bagpipes. It was impossible to look away from these tall figures, as they twirled and swayed through the choreography. The end of the dance was marked by booming applause, as the 150-year-old puppets took a rest. The innocent joy of the laughing youngsters stirred childhood recollections of watching the Santa Claus Parade with her father, on the snowy streets of Toronto.

Lost in a cherished memory, Lily thought she saw Miguel across the street. Her body became tense, as her eyes focussed on the individual. *Is it him?* Circling in the opposite direction, Lily's initial impulse was to leave. Spotting him again, she abruptly stopped. Miguel looked distressed as he darted through the crowd—something was not right.

Sudden worry coated her thoughts. "I see one of my colleagues, Lucas. I'll be right back." Weaving through, Lily approached and gently tapped Miguel's shoulder. Only then did she realize Lucas was right behind her. Yelling over the bagpipes, she couldn't walk away. "Is everything okay?" Miguel's brows furrowed over his pale face.

Pushing forward, Lucas forcefully grabbed her arm. "Let's go, Lily." Without warning, with a single punch Miguel knocked Lucas to the ground. A bolt of shock coiled through Lily's chest.

"Miguel! What are you doing?!!" She couldn't read his face. His watery brown eyes projected anger and worry.

Lily quickly turned her attention to the man on the ground. "Are you okay??" Lucas shook his head as he wobbled to his feet, his hand cupping his eye.

Seizing her arm, Lucas gritted, "Let's get out of here."

"Wait—" She shrugged him off for the last time and approached Miguel. "*What* is going on?!"

"I'm leaving *now* Lily." Lucas cleared out when she made no move to join him.

Speaking rapidly, Miguel paused to catch his breath. "I can't find Amaya, Lily. She was a bit frightened by the Kilikis, but I encouraged her to get closer. She reluctantly joined the other kids and—I lost sight of her. I can't find her!"

"She can't be far, Miguel." With an intense adrenaline boost, the two of them scoured the crowd into which Lucas had disappeared. Their voices became hoarse, yelling, "Amaya!!!!". All of the children were wearing identical colours, so Lily focussed on Amaya's straight chestnut hair. With the parade moving along the street, she pushed away the nerves settling in her stomach. *Think clearly.*

"What about the ice cream shop we passed?" Lily dashed over as a speechless Miguel tagged behind. Surveying the line, Lily's chest became numb.

Observing his trembling body, she held his shoulder. He pulled away, snubbing her touch. "Slow your breathing, Miguel. We are going to find her." Nodding, he pointed to a nearby park. "Good idea. She loves the swings." Lily's sprint left Miguel well behind. *No Amaya.*

Retracing their steps, they combed the area with military precision for another hour. It was time to get some help.

"Are you sure you shouldn't contact someone? Your mom or Amaya's father, maybe?" Miguel sat motionless with his forearms resting on his knees, and his tortured head braced in his hands. The rattling fan hardly moved the stale air in the narrow yellow office. Waiting for the police officer, for over an hour, Miguel persisted in his silence as Lily memorized the contents of the beige desk. Her eyes had outlined the huge printer, pile of papers, computer, another stack of papers, and a telephone, innumerable times. The bulletin board's public service posters were also seared into her brain. Her patience evaporated.

Lily dragged her chair to face Miguel. "I really think you should reach out to your family."

He lifted his head and wiping his moist eyes, twisted to grab his cigarette pack. "I'm such a screw-up. I can't even keep my niece safe on a simple outing. She has to be okay. How can this be happening?" Lily snatched the Marlboro pack and tossed it on the desk. She swung in closer, locking her knees to Miguel's, and placed her hands around his, calming the shaking. This time he didn't pull back.

"Amaya is a smart kid. I'm sure she wandered off and has figured out how to get home. I know your mobile is dead, but you can call from here." Lily's head moved in the direction of the desk phone. She could not comprehend Miguel's hesitation to call home.

Raising his voice, Miguel responded. "I can't bring *more* harm to my family." He grounded his head and a fleet of emotions set sail. "My sister is in the hospital because of me."

He released his hands from hers and snatched the cigarettes from the desk. "It was an accident on an icy road. How can that be your fault, Miguel?"

His brown eyes grew wide and appeared haunted as he spoke. "My ex-girlfriend was trying to reconcile things between us." A guilty relief washed over Lily to hear him say *ex*-girlfriend—this detail had been conveniently left out by Lucas. "We had broken up in the summer after she cheated on me with your *date*, and I hadn't seen her in months. I ran into her at a mutual friend's place at Christmas, and *she* decided we needed to be together. I didn't feel that way, but there was no stopping her. She convinced my sister to use the B&B for a romantic dinner she was going to prepare. Isabel was driving her when the accident happened."

Regretting every minute she had spent with Lucas, Lily's heart shattered for this tormented man. "I'm so sorry Miguel, but the accident was not your fault. No one would blame *you* for this."

"I blame myself. I had a role in this, somehow. Susana *died*." He violently shook his head. The pain appeared to harden as he spoke. "And ... Isabel's life has changed forever because she believed she was doing something special for her brother. Now, Amaya, entrusted to me, is missing."

Lily's brain multitasked as she processed his words. Miguel's wrist tattoo was *not* for Susana—she had misjudged the entire situation.

"Please, call your mom." Oblivious to her words, Miguel's confessions continued.

"When my father died, instead of caring for my family, I escaped to the UK for six months and partied—hard. What kind of person *does* such a thing?" Tears rolled from the corners of his eyes.

Taking a tissue from her purse, Lily swabbed the droplets from his tired cheek. "Everyone grieves differently. You need to be kinder to yourself, Miguel. We all make mistakes." His face relaxed somewhat, perhaps soothed by voicing these confessions.

Firmly passing the handset into Miguel's hand, Lily's eyes pleaded with him. As Miguel pulsed the numbers into the telephone, a thin sheet of calmness draped the office. "Mamá." He spoke quickly, but his face transformed as he listened. Colour flushed back, and his wide smile radiated. She could stare at his face forever.

Hanging up the telephone, he flopped back into the chair yelling. "Amaya is safe!" Joyful tears gushed over their tense faces. Miguel tenderly squeezed Lily's hand.

Allowing his head to fall back, his voice was euphoric. "She saw her cousins and Tía at the parade and went off with them. I guess I was moving around so quickly they couldn't find me, to let me know. My mother is going to contact Sara and ask her to bring Amaya here."

Lily leapt, stretching her stiff legs. "That's the best news, Miguel. You can salvage the rest of the day with Amaya." Miguel nodded as he rose.

"What does the rest of your day look like? Are you going to meet up with Lucas?" His voice betrayed a tinge of jealousy.

"And offer him more first-aid?" Miguel's cheeks flushed with embarrassment. Miguel decking Lucas was shocking but understanding the context smoothed away some of the rawness.

"This isn't the time and place to talk about that, Lily. Just promise to be careful with him. He's not a good person." His serious face made a cameo.

Studying his reaction as she spoke, Lily locked her eyes. "I'm not sure what I plan to do today but I will be careful." A shallow smile crossed his mouth and his face lightened.

Lily tried to squash the fluttery sensations in her chest and stomach. After this harrowing episode, she knew their bond had deepened—but nothing substantial had changed. An empty feeling set in.

"Tío!" Amaya stormed into the office and flung herself into Miguel's arms. He raised the child up high and twirled her around like a pinwheel.

Still tearing up, his joy was infectious. "You scared me so much, amor." He glanced at Lily as she quietly slipped through the office door.

The sweltering heat of that eventful day subsided as a temperate evening set in. Slipping off his barstool outside of the Bodegón, Miguel's excitement charged the patio. "Isabel looked very nervous … but the moment Amaya saw her and screamed her name, the awkwardness melted away! It was beautiful to watch." Antonio raised his wine to toast the wonderful news.

"I think this will help both of them." Slapping Miguel's shoulder, Antonio's grin widened.

Recalling the afternoon energized his already jubilant mood. "Amaya was unbelievable with her. She massaged her legs and helped Isabel take some steps with the walker. She curled up with her mom and rubbed her back, as Isabel napped."

"It sounds like you hit an all-time low in the morning, followed by an all-time high in the afternoon!" Antonio had described his day precisely. Miguel nodded, as he swallowed the last bite of his anchovy toast.

"I don't want to even think about the morning. I was in a state of panic."

Antonio wiped his mouth and placed the serviette by his wine. Tilting his head to better read Miguel's face, he lobbed a delicate subject. "I find it incredible that Lily was there. What are the odds?"

Miguel beamed, hearing her name. "I don't even think Lily realizes she got me through one of the toughest moments of my life." Then, pressing his lips together, it all came rushing back, and

Miguel's mood instantly morphed. "But ... she wasn't alone." A wave of anger invaded his chest.

Antonio dropped his head. "When they went for coffee yesterday, I didn't know that my cousin and Lily had made plans to see each other again."

"That's what I thought ... It goes without saying that they met at the *welcoming* Arco Íris." A vein by Miguel's temple twitched as he responded—a unique variety of hurt took hold when he envisioned Lucas with Lily. Together.

Antonio took off his glasses and set them down on the table. He rubbed the bridge of his nose. "What is that supposed to mean?"

"Why does that jerk even work for you? You know what he did." There—he had finally said it! Having festered for a year, the release felt liberating.

"I'm sorry that—"

Miguel cut him off before he could complete his thought. "Forget it, Antonio. I have no right telling you how to run your business." *Not here Miguel.* He patted his best friend's shoulder and raised his glass, hoping he could wash away the friction, but Miguel's resentment remained.

Antonio's eyebrows lifted. "So ... how did you leave things with Lily?" His tone was artificially light. The tension between them remained.

"She left when Amaya arrived. I don't even think I thanked her for being there and getting me through this nightmare." *Who's the jerk now?* "She looked appalled when I punched Lucas but then took control when we searched for Amaya."

Shaking his head, Antonio's frustration was visible. "What? ... When are you seeing her again?"

"I'm not. Nothing has changed Antonio. I missed my chance with her."

Rubbing the back of his neck, Antonio drilled down. "Don't tell me nothing has changed! You don't go through an experience like this, without it bringing you closer."

Attempting to sound calm, Miguel's voice was firm. "Please leave it alone, Antonio. This is what she wants." A burning sensation settled in Miguel's chest. He could not hide his sad eyes.

Dani joined them on the patio, clutching their shoulders. "Which table should I reserve for the final game tomorrow? How many of you are coming? When does Bea return?"

Antonio's blissful face said it all. "She gets back tonight."

Dani elbowed Miguel. "Make sure he has some energy left tomorrow to cheer on La Roja!" Miguel struggled to flash a smile. He couldn't avert the anger he felt towards his oldest friend.

Sharing in the laughter, Antonio stroked his beard. "I think a table for six will work."

"Muy bien. Can I get you two more wine?" Dani wiped the tiled surface of the table.

"I'm fine. I need to get back to Puente." He hopped off the stool. "Save a table for five, Dani. I won't be coming." He pivoted and stormed down the street while Antonio shouted for him to return.

CHAPTER THIRTEEN

The wind was calm, and the early morning sun sizzled. Lily's jog was strenuous this Sunday morning, the perfect opportunity to blow off some steam. She felt out of shape because of the overdrinking and overeating of the last few days. Her camp classes resumed at the end of the week. As she controlled her breathing and pacing, Lily realized she needed to rejoin her companions *structure* and *routine* and say goodbye to the spontaneity she had sampled during the Festival.

Outside of the café, a patio table and two chairs were set up. Closed during San Fermín, Lily was puzzled. As she approached, Cristina greeted her outside the magenta door.

"Lily! Que sorpresa." Cristina hugged her tightly. "Water or café?" Lily's red cheeks and perspired T-shirt answered for her.

Plunking herself on the bistro chair, she caught her breath. "Are you open today?"

"No. I come to put water for my flowers and to think." She stroked Lily's cheek with much affection. "How do you like San Fermín? Do you enjoy?" Admiring the flowers spilling from the box planters, Lily considered her answer.

"Yes. Pamplona has shown me a great deal." Gulping the water, she dabbed the serviette across her face. "What about you, Cristina? Is everything okay?"

Stirring her coffee slowly, she cleared her throat. "I am confused today. I want to sell my father's casa rural, but I don't know. The familia needs money, but my children no like the idea. A real estate guy is coming to the house tomorrow." Cristina shrugged her shoulders. The skin around her forehead bunched.

Lily's steady eyes tried to comfort. "Well, you shouldn't feel rushed. A real estate agent can give you an appraisal, but you can still think about it, and talk to your children."

"My children will not sell. It is a beautiful casa. Two hundred years old. The small town is very especial too. I want you to visitar." Cristina's face softened as she spoke of the home.

Without delay, Lily jumped at the invitation. "I would love to see it. A relaxing day in the country would clear my head." Her dull eyes fixated on the silver ring she nervously rotated.

Tilting her head to lean forward, Cristina's eyes grilled Lily's face. "Why is you head no clear? Boy problema?"

"Yes." Lily giggled sheepishly. "I met a wonderful, complicated man. We share a real connection, but he hurt me, and I walked away. Now … I can't get him out of my head."

Standing, Cristina patted Lily's knee. "The heart is no easy to control, bonita." Nodding, Lily kissed her cheeks and hit the pavement. "Good luck with the casa rural. I'll be back this week."

Cristina's fatigued arm waved adiós.

Clasping hands, Miguel strolled towards Antonio's desk with an excited Amaya. The bookstore was closed to the public on Sunday but open to family and friends.

"Hi, Antonio! Mamá said I could get three books." Lifting her off the ground with a twirl, Antonio was delighted to see her.

"I will gift you one, so pick out four books, sweetheart." Antonio landed a loud kiss on Amaya, and her feet hit the floor. Cheering, the young girl skipped off to the forest of book stacks.

"Amaya looks so happy." Miguel did not respond, just nodded passively.

Antonio carefully manoeuvred between the four boxes in front of his desk. The snap of the utility knife freed the contents inside. "Are you ok? What happened last night?"

Miguel could feel his facial muscles tightening up. "I'm done talking Antonio. My sister asked me to bring Amaya here to select some books and that's it."

Antonio's perplexed look signalled more commentary to come. "I don't understand. Your sister and niece are in a very good place now and you are walking around so pissed with the world. Talk to me."

The blood rushed down his cheeks as Miguel scanned the bookstore. "Is Lucas in? I need to talk to him."

"I don't think that's a good idea, Miguel." Antonio rounded his desk to come closer.

"Still protecting him?" The feeling of betrayal dug deep even though Miguel understood well the tether of family ties.

Throwing his hands up Antonio looked overwhelmed. "No! I mean, Amaya is just over there."

"I'm aware."

Antonio walked away, looking disappointed. "You need to get your shit together, Miguel."

Spotting Lucas dragging a dolly with two large boxes, he dashed toward him. Lucas saw him coming. He put down the packing slip and stood erect, crossing his arms, legs in a wide stance. "Did you come back for more? At least this time it would be a fairer fight." Miguel stared at him, thinking the black eye suited him well. "I guess you couldn't handle yummy Lily wanting to be with *me*."

You disrespectful ass. Showing the whites of his eyes, adrenaline rushed through Miguel's body. He leaned towards Lucas forcefully. "Don't ever talk about her that way."

Chuckling unpleasantly, Lucas rolled his eyes. "Why so touchy? *You* aren't dating her."

"That didn't stop you before." Miguel's cheeks burned, and his throat was dry from the rushed breathing.

Lucas's mouth smirked. "Ancient history, my friend. Move on." Miguel had put the ugly affair behind him, but confronting Lucas still felt good.

"Things were essentially over between the two of us when Susana made her way to your bed." Guilt rushed through his chest as he spoke negatively about the deceased. "This ancient history taught me all I need to know about you, Lucas."

"I'm sure it did. I know how to cherish a wonderful woman." Puffing out his chest, Lucas fixed his gaze on Miguel's frowning eyes. "I *will* get better acquainted with Lily."

Miguel pressed his fist against his breastbone, as jealousy and anger pelted through.

Antonio stepped forward, obstructing Miguel's path to Lucas. "You're my best friend, Antonio. You need to step aside before I do something I will regret."

Defeated, Antonio moved away as Miguel turned towards Lucas. Knowing that his niece was close by restrained the fallout. Tapping his index finger on Lucas's collarbone, Miguel's red face drew in. "If you hurt her, you better watch your back."

Pacing towards the door, Miguel called out to his niece. "Amaya, vamos."

Below the beamed ceiling, the tension dangled and clung to the patrons of the Bodegón. The hot moisture in the air intensified the anxious mood. With a scoreless match, the World Cup final was headed towards extra time. The bar, saturated in red jerseys, pounded with each play. Two brave Dutch fans, perched at the bar, confused the colour scheme with their orange shirts.

Fergus provided animated commentary for the table, as Jade, and Beatriz swapped Zurich stories. Antonio seemed distracted and agitated, not focussing on the biggest football match Spain had ever played. Lily was also unusually quiet, her unease, a combination of game-time nerves, and confusion. Nodding and smiling at the appropriate moments in the conversation, her contemplations kept her busy.

Dani replaced the pitcher of sangría and delivered a platter of calamares fritos. He frowned at the table as he passed. "¿Donde está tu sonrisa? I need to see your beautiful smile Lily—and you, too, Antonio! Why so glum? Spain is playing well, amigo!"

Blushing, Lily's grin was wide and bright. Antonio reluctantly put his hand up for a high five and regained some colour in his face.

Beatriz filled their wine glasses and signalled for Lily to join her outside. Without heels, she was close to Lily's height. Her short auburn curls and sapphire-blue eyes were gorgeous. Lily had met Beatriz a few hours ago and instantly warmed to her candid and easygoing nature.

Swinging her pack of cigarettes, Beatriz placed the wine glass on the bistro table. "Would you like one?"

Lily smirked at the offer, recalling Miguel's nervous habit. Beatriz lit up and channelled Lily's thoughts, exhaling a puff of smoke. "At least I smoke and don't play with the package, like my good friend." She winked at Lily and gulped the sangría. "I'm sorry things didn't work out. He is a bit messed up right now."

Lily's mouth fell open. Before she could respond, Beatriz put her arm around her. "I have known Miguel since I was five. I love him like a brother and in my family, we tell the truth." Lily nodded and braced herself for Beatriz's analysis. "I hear you two have much chemistry. Until you return home, you should enjoy each other. Maybe you need to open up, bonita."

Lily drew in a breath and calmly released it before speaking. "I'm very skilled at building protective walls, but I'll think about what you said." Beatriz had put it so simply. Was it possible for her to trust Miguel, again? "We should get back. I don't want to miss the second half of extra time." Beatriz put out her cigarette and arm-in-arm they returned to the match.

A cautious hush came over the table as they approached. Peering at Jade and Fergus, Lily's curiosity grew. "What's going on?"

"I have a lovely surprise for you, darling." Jade exuded confidence, while Fergus shrugged his shoulders, eyes glued on the television screen.

It was at this moment, Andrés Iniesta scored for Spain. The bar went wild. Euphoric jumping and chanting took over. With a few minutes left in the game, the dream of Spain winning its first World Cup rocked the bar.

Dani leapt onto the counter and twirled his bar mop. Antonio shed joyful tears, as Beatriz, and Fergus danced around the table. Jade stood and observed the reaction like an anthropologist studying a remote tribe. Lily joined in the song of "Campeones! Campeones! Olé! Olé! Olé!" as the conga line snaked through the Bodegón and out to the street. The party would not end until daybreak.

CHAPTER FOURTEEN

Lily's pounding headache was starting to subside. Drinking another bottle of water seemed to help her celebratory hangover. She had barely managed to put together an overnight bag and drape on her cropped coral racerback and denim shorts. Oddly, Lily had accepted Jade's surprise gift of a country getaway, without the usual discussion of paying her share. Hidden behind her black aviator sunglasses, her head lounging on the window of the taxi door, Lily leafed through the guidebook of northern Spain.

"Wow … Puente La Reina has a six-arched bridge, dating back to the eleventh century."

Clicking the keyboard, Jade returned company emails as she conversed with Lily. "The town is a medieval gem." One would never know Jade had participated in the evening celebrations. Her golden hair was expertly groomed and not a speck of fatigue appeared on her face—she looked radiant in her white sleeveless linen dress. Her one concession today was wearing flat sandals.

"Thanks again for this overnight trip, Jade. It's exactly what I need. Seeing Miguel on Saturday was difficult."

Lily noticed Jade's sly smile. "Are you sure you don't want to give Mr. Serious another chance?" Shrugging her shoulders, a blanket of confusion wrapped around her. Avoiding the question, Lily tightly squeezed Jade's hand as she changed the conversation.

"I'm sad you are leaving in four days. The month flew by!"

Sounding uncommonly sincere, Jade smiled back. "I'm very happy I came."

The taxi stopped in the driveway of a charming inn. As they stepped out, the fresh country air supplied pep to Lily's tired body. Chirping birds flew over the wood shingles of the sloped roof. The whitewashed front of the home was accented by dark brown woodwork and stone. The balcony planters burst with red geraniums.

A mahogany desk, in a large common room, served as the check-in counter. The modern touches to this rustic farmhouse were striking.

"Hello. Welcome to Casa Emi. My name is Elena." The exceedingly friendly woman, processed their documents, grabbed their bags, and swiftly escorted them to their room. Lily was in awe of her strength and speed.

Jade crossed her arms as she surveyed the room. "Not my usual standard, but it will do."

The dark wood floors matched the ceiling beams of the bedroom. Stone wainscoting adorned the white walls. The handmade quilt on the double bed featured floral squares, in a variety of blue tones.

"I think it's enchanting." Pink wildflowers sat on the modest dresser, beside the heavy wood armchair. Lily rested her bag below the curtain that danced in the breeze of the open window. She felt at home.

"The washroom is completely renovated. Thank goodness!" Jade launched her leather tote over her shoulder. "Let's go sightseeing."

Setting the fabric mesh bags onto the kitchen counter, Miguel robotically put away the fresh produce from the town's market. His thoughts whirled like a Category 5 hurricane. He felt numb, regretting his aggression towards Lucas and Antonio ... how could he alienate the only friend who had stood by him this last year? And Lily … that ache was profound. *What a screw-up!*

The ramekins of natillas, a favourite pudding of the Morneau couple, would have to be refrigerated, for their last night at the B&B. Miguel tried to focus as he placed the extra vanilla custards in the fridge but was not surprised when two of them crashed onto the dark wood floor. *What else?* He picked up the glass fragments, piercing his thumb.

As he secured the band-aid, the scent of apricots and plums Miguel had arranged in the ceramic fruit bowl, woke up his stomach. He had not eaten most of yesterday, but lunch would have to wait until his unsolicited visitor left. Miguel was not pleased to be touring the real estate agent, but he had promised his mother to be civil. This was not his day. Could he ever catch a break?

The patio would also need straightening, after last night's World Cup party. He had relished the victory with his guests but regretted his absence from the Bodegón. Rubbing his father's name tattooed on his wrist, Miguel wondered if Papá would be disappointed that he missed seeing Spain, at their sacred place, playing a World Cup final.

Vacuuming the common room, Elena hollered, "Did you remember the laundry detergent?"

Scrubbing his hand over his face, Miguel shook his head. "I knew I forgot something!" Entering the common room, Miguel straightened out some papers on the check-in desk and picked through the mail. "I can go now."

"No rush. I still have half a bottle left."

Blinking rapidly, Miguel fixated on the guest registry: *Jade Allen and Lily Harrison.* His stomach dropped. Flying out the back door, he could hear Elena. "I don't need the detergent, Miguel!"

Overcome by nervous energy, Miguel vigorously swept the patio, lost in thought. A cocktail of longing and confusion stirred through his head. The sale of the B&B, as well as the uncertain future of his family, had cooled his steady thoughts of Lily. Distance from her had kept him focussed. *Now this*! Their visit to the B&B reeked of Antonio. Maybe he could go back to Pamplona now? But the real estate appointment could not be rescheduled. His mother would kill him! On the other hand, maybe it was time to confront Lily about Lucas.

Elena stepped outside with a glass of water, flopping onto the periwinkle recliner. "Oh good! I thought you had left."

"I see we have two new guests." Miguel tried to look relaxed as he inquired.

She winked at him, stretching her legs. "Yes. Two beautiful women, Miguel."

"Will they be back soon or are they out for the day?" Rubbing her chin, Elena looked puzzled. "I mean … I wouldn't want them to be here when the real estate agent is touring the property." Miguel was satisfied with his deception.

"Right. I can ask them to come back a bit later."

Having bought himself some time, Miguel could breathe.

Jade's mouth fell open, as Lily ordered their lunch in perfect Spanish. "Impressive."

Lily flashed a knowing grin. She had been studying her Spanish verbs from a book she borrowed from Alegría. Timid to speak to Spaniards she knew, Lily practiced with shopkeepers and waiters. "So … what did you order?"

Lily listed the menu with the confidence of an experienced maître d'. "To start, we are sharing white asparagus in a sherry vinaigrette and a white bean vegetable stew called pochas. Then, you will be enjoying the grilled lamb chops while I indulge in piquillo red peppers stuffed with cod. Silky flan has been ordered for dessert."

Jade's Hollywood smile emerged. "I approve." The waiter served the chilled rosé, and the two friends clinked their wine glasses in honour of this special day at Puente La Reina.

"This wine is delicious. It's one of Fergus's favourites." Jade's cheeks blushed, as she placed her glass.

Lily pulled her chair in closer. "So, what's the deal with you two?"

"I need to get back to work, but I'm hoping to spend a week with him in Edinburgh in the fall."

Clapping her hands, Lily was thrilled to hear the news. With a decisive nod, her eyes fixed on Jade. "It's certainly more than a summer fling, right?"

Jade's steel blue eyes sparkled. "We talked yesterday. Long-distance relationships are a tricky endeavour, but we are committed to making it work. More travel in my future, but it suits me fine." A flash of envy was extinguished by the joy Lily felt for her oldest friend.

Raising her glass, she toasted. "A measly ocean couldn't break the magic you two share." The waiter arrived with the first course, as Jade blew Lily a kiss.

Needing to walk off the delicious meal, the women strolled the main street. "I've never visited so many churches in my life." Jade winked as she drew out her scarlet fan.

"The Church of the Crucifix is my favourite. I loved the stone arch over the huge wooden doors. It's so peaceful inside."

"The one founded by the Knight Templars, with the hospital for the pilgrims beside it, right?" Pleased Jade had been listening to her historical commentary, Lily nodded and patted her friend on the back, as they made their way towards the ancient bridge.

Passing countless pilgrims with their backpacks, hiking shoes, sun hats, and wooden walking sticks, the greeting "buen camino" or "good journey," was commonplace. "Pilgrims have walked these *exact* streets for over one thousand years." Lily's eyes watered, overcome with emotion and connection.

Jade shook her head. "I don't know how they do it. That's far too much walking for me! I'm sure I would get lost."

"The Camino shell would direct you." Lily pointed at the marker painted on a tree. The scallop shape was printed in yellow on a blue background above a yellow arrow indicating the route to follow. They had seen these unique signs everywhere throughout the town, on sidewalks, milestones, wall tiles, and trees.

Browsing at a gift shop, Lily purchased two souvenirs: a natural scallop shell for Cristina's café and a small charm for herself. Clipping it to her bracelet, Lily counted on the silver shell to guide her camino.

As they approached the B&B, Elena came rushing along the driveway. "Hello! I hope you had a wonderful day?"

Quite the welcome, thought Lily.

"We did, thank you," Jade was quick to respond.

Stretching out her arms, Lily's few hours of sleep had finally caught up with her. "I think I need a siesta." The receptionist's forehead wrinkled.

"Oh no ... the owner of the inn is showing his real estate agent the property and has asked all guests to give him a bit more time before returning to the B&B."

Biting her lip, Jade asked an odd question. "The owner is here?"

"Yes. Well ... the real owner is his mother. They have already visited the patio. You could lie on one of the lounge chairs, Señorita Harrison. I have taken many naps there." *His mother is the owner?* Lily had tuned out most of Elena's words, after hearing this.

Bouncing from foot to foot, Lily could not contain her excitement. "Elena, is the owner's name Cristina?" Taking a step back, Jade's bewildered face caught her eye. "You know, Jade ... the lovely owner of the café I visit in the morning."

Sharing in this serendipitous moment, Elena's voice was bubbly. "Yes! Her name is Cristina."

"I can't believe this. I saw her yesterday morning, and we talked about her selling the casa rural. I didn't realize it was a B&B." Rattling her head, she grabbed Jade's arm. "I would love to meet her son!"

As they rambled towards the patio, Jade closed her eyes and lowered her head. "Lil ... I need to tell you something." Settling on the two recliners facing a patch of wild foxgloves, Lily got comfy. The periwinkle cushion was firm beneath her fatigued body. Elena was right. Napping here would be easy.

Her eyelids were beginning to slope as she fixed the headrest. "What's wrong, Jade?"

"You know the owner's son." Jade exhaled dramatically. "It's Miguel."

A frenzy of emotions rushed through Lily's body as her chest tightened. *Cristina is Miguel's mother?* She spun her legs around and faced Jade.

"What?!"

In a pleading voice, Jade confessed, "I wanted to give you an opportunity to see Miguel before I left, to be sure you made the right decision about him. I don't know what I'm doing, frankly. My feelings for Fergus are making me a bit sappy these days. I knew Miguel would be working here today, so I booked this getaway. Don't be upset."

Lily dropped back on the recliner and said nothing. She needed to unravel her tangled sentiments.

After some time, she sluggishly sat and gave Jade a hug. "I know you meant well. You are right—I have strong feelings for Miguel ... and I also wonder if I made the right decision. Jade, when he walked away from me, it hurt so much! My life has been filled with people leaving me. You know that. I'm trying to put an end to it."

Releasing the embrace, Lily stared at the one person who was always present in her life. "I'm going to take a walk. I'll be back soon—but I won't be seeing Miguel."

Jade kissed Lily's forehead. "No more meddling; I promise."

CHAPTER FIFTEEN

Miguel shook hands with the agent. He hadn't expected to like him. "I will be in touch shortly. This is a difficult decision. I wish your family all the best, as you sort through options."

Waving, as the car pulled away, Elena walked towards Miguel. "How did it go?"

"I think I have it figured out!" Grabbing Elena's arm, Miguel eagerly outlined his plan. "I will convince my mother to wait a few weeks to list the property. On Monday, Isa will be discharged, and I'll bring her to Puente with Amaya. Once my mother realizes how important this place is to my sister's recovery, she won't want to sell."

Elena's face tightened as her brows drew closer. Cutting in on her negativity, Miguel's eyes pleaded. "Please support me with this."

Answering with a small nod, Elena's arm encircled his back. "Of course. Now ... can I let the guests back in?"

Kneading the back of his neck, Miguel now focussed on his unexpected visitors. "Sure. I hope no one was upset about this."

"Not at all. Most of the guests have not returned yet. Señorita Harrison needed a nap, but I think she left. Señorita Allen is the only one waiting at the patio." Hearing Lily's name, his stomach rippled.

"I'll let Señorita Allen know, Elena. You should get back home. Thanks for staying."

Entering the kitchen, Miguel removed the intact natillas from the refrigerator. Mr. Morneau preferred his custard at room temperature. Sprinkling ground cinnamon, he placed the ramekins on a hammered iron tray. Adding a small glass vase with pink wildflowers and a farewell card, his last task of the day was completed.

Noisily dragging out the garden chair, Miguel hoped to wake his tired guest. He sat at a distance, as she appeared startled to see him.

Sitting up, Jade wiped her eyes. "Hello, Miguel. It's so peaceful here. I guess I nodded off."

"Hi, Jade. Welcome to Casa Emi. This is a surprise. I didn't know you two were coming." His cool stare betrayed his warm salutation.

Chewing the inside of her mouth, Jade's eyes narrowed. "That was intentional, Miguel."

"I figured. Antonio won't let it go." Tapping his feet, he wrestled his cigarettes from his back pocket.

Looking up, Jade squinted sternly. "Actually, this was all my doing. I casually asked Antonio for the name of your B&B. He has no idea we are here."

Regretting his conflicted thoughts towards his friend, Miguel sat motionless, gripping the Marlboro pack.

"I clearly made a mistake. I'm sorry, Miguel. I had no right to push Lily and you into this situation. We'll be out of your way tomorrow."

Her words stung. He was secretly grateful for this unexpected meeting. With a shaky voice and vacant stare, Miguel stood. "Good ... well, thanks for your honesty, Jade."

Squeezing his shoulder as she walked towards the door, Jade nodded. "By the way, Lily knows your mother."

Taking a cleansing breath, Miguel looked baffled. "How?"

"She jogs by the café in the mornings. They have become quite close."

Stomach churning, Miguel felt utterly depleted. He wished this surreal day would end.

Lily spied Miguel chatting with an older couple, as she dashed through the hall, adjacent to the common room. A cheesy game show aired on the television. The audio was unusually high. She calmly greeted the room as she swept by. "Buenas noches."

Her thirst had ballooned, after the three-hour tour along the banks of the River Arga. She planned to grab some water from the kitchen and disappear upstairs. After washing her hands in the white clay sink, Lily ran the cold water. The soft dish towel was infused with Miguel's cologne. Her chest fluttered as she held it to her nose and breathed him in. Filling a tall glass, the scent of cinnamon in the kitchen reminded her of Thanksgiving baking.

"Hi, Lily." A guarded smile crossed her face, as Miguel entered the kitchen.

Her breath quickened as she spoke. "Miguel ... I didn't have anything to do with this visit."

"I know." His eyes looked blankly at her. "I didn't think you would be interested in visiting me, now that you and Lucas have found each other."

Decisively clenching the glass, Lily faced the stairs. She had no time for this nonsense. "I'm going to sleep now, and we'll be gone in the morning."

"I can recommend some romantic local spots the two of you can visit." Lightly kicking the baseboard, Miguel's voice filled the kitchen. Lily stopped abruptly. *Enough!*

Swallowing before speaking, Lily turned to face him, droplets of sweat collecting on her forehead. "So let me get this straight. You made it abundantly clear that you have no interest in me and my *overstepping* tendencies, and yet you seem acutely interested in my relationship with Lucas. Am I correct?"

Miguel moved closer. His chocolate brown eyes become glossy. "I'm not interested in your relationship with Lucas." His voice softened and he spoke slowly. "I'm just trying to tell you that you need to be careful with him."

"Why do you even care, Miguel?" Pulling at her ponytail, Lily was exhausted.

Mrs. Morneau popped her head into the kitchen. "I don't mean to be rude, dears, but could you keep your voices down? Mr. Morneau is having a hard time hearing the show."

Assaulted by the blaring volume of the television, Miguel and Lily gave each other a puzzled glance. A hairline fracture briefly cracked the tension between them.

"Of course, Mrs. Morneau. I'm sorry." Miguel seized Lily's free hand and ferried her towards the hall. Shrugging her hand away she felt the spark of his touch. Reluctantly Lily followed Miguel into the family studio.

Lily stood by the plush white sofa tapping her leg and clasping her hands tightly as her palm still tingled from the warmth of the touch. Miguel switched on the floor lamp, flooding the room with a golden hue. The cozy studio was positioned off the common room of the B&B, where the television was still broadcasting in Dolby surround sound. An arched stone wall divided the living area and kitchenette from the bedroom. Lily scanned the space, noticing the clothes tossed onto a poorly made bed. Dishes gathered in the sink. The apartment had a relaxing vibe; the opposite of how she was feeling.

Bringing this discussion to an end, Lily got to the point. "Well, Miguel? Why do you care enough to comment on my relationship with Lucas?" Aware of her pounding heartbeat, Lily pushed through.

Miguel paced like a caged animal. "You are a good person, with a big heart, Lily … and I don't want to see you get hurt." He looked down, slowing his stride stopping close to her reminding Lily of when he pressed her to the railing of the balcony above Estafeta.

Catching her breath Lily tried to focus. "I know how to take care of myself, Miguel. I've been doing it—solo—for most of my life. Give me a bit more credit." Lily's chest perked, as her eyebrows scrunched.

She could see his firm chest swelling beneath his light T-shirt. "Why do you always react this way, Lily? That's not what I meant." Her cheeks rushed with heat. "Always?" Moving slowly towards the door, she shook her head. This argument was going nowhere. "I have absolutely no interest in Lucas. It was a mistake to spend *any* time with him ... Good night, Miguel."

As she held the doorknob, Miguel's hand covered her fist. Standing inches behind, he buried his face in the nape of her neck and whispered, "Please stay."

Lily stood frozen, facing the door. The intensity of his breath, streaming over her bare neck, pooled with the heat of his body. Her muscles turned to mush as her good sense and caution flew out of her head at his touch.

She briskly turned and met his full lips, the ones she'd dreamed about since that morning in Jade's studio. He tasted like cinnamon as he spread the spice along her lips with his generous tongue. Lily clutched his hair as he pressed her against the wall. Every nerve in her body was humming, as he licked and nibbled on her ear.

She tracked her hands under his T-shirt, caressing his toned chest, memorizing the texture and shape. His groans made her head spin. Peeling off his shirt, the warmth of his body, and his citrus scent, draped over her. His pounding heart vibrated between them, then his mouth settled over hers, their tongues rushing to entwine. He lifted her tank top, skimming his thumbs over her lace bra, caressing her heaving chest. Fondling her hair, he removed the elastic. Tresses cascaded over her bare shoulders.

As Miguel skillfully kissed the curve of her throat, Lily's head fell back. He unfastened her bra, tasting her breasts, teeth tugging at her hard nipples. A bolt of electricity surged. Her tongue swirled his earlobe, as her fingers unbuttoned his jeans. They dropped as her hand felt the swelling. Pulling him in closer, she cast off his boxers, cupping his firm buttocks.

Miguel placed his arm around her waist and lifted her from the floor. Wrapping her legs around him, Lily bit his wild lips.

Miguel settled her on the bed, studying her body with his mouth and hands, as he made his way below her navel. Every curve and dip was attended to, as Lily's body rocketed in ecstasy.

Slipping off her shorts and panties, Miguel continued to explore. Lily's moans grew louder, as his fingers moved skillfully inside her, pressing and swirling. Her back arched as his tongue drove the exhilaration to a new level; her legs flexed against his smooth back, as Miguel's sable hair tickled her inner thighs. Lily's body was writhing and curving with pleasure, as his tongue worked quickly. Grasping the bed sheets, she pulled them into knots.

Climaxing, Lily's body boldly quivered as she let out a cry. Miguel sprung onto the bed, moulding his body to hers, as he brushed her dewy hair from her glowing face.

Lily pushed Miguel onto his back and straddled him—his skin was flushed with excitement. Tilting his head back, he closed his eyes, and cupped her breasts, sensually moving his palms in a semicircle. Lily kissed his mouth hard as she rotated her hips, skimming his groin.

She gently bit his neck and coated his chest with searing kisses. Slithering down his moist body, she placed her mouth over him. He let out a raw grunt as her lips moved up and down and her fingers massaged his swollen sack. Her body tingled, feeling his arousal heighten.

Guiding her upwards, Miguel seized her mouth hungrily as she flipped on her back. Lily's fit legs swaddled his body as he thrust into her. The long slow strokes were robust and deep, sending her to an unknown, blissful place.

His eyes, dark with desire, glowed.

Quickening the pace, he dove into her, again, and again. They moaned together, lost in a web of pleasure. Digging her fingers into his back, a rush of sensations thundered over Lily, until it crested, leaving her weightless. She caught her breath, sensing the warmth of his climax. Miguel shuddered and trembled, then crumbled over her slender body.

Struggling for air, Miguel cradled her. "¡Que divino!" He cupped her face, and Lily was stirred by the genuine tenderness of Miguel's kiss. They lay facing each other in silence, their bodies glued together, hands clasped, eyes locked and noses gently brushing. Lily gently floated back to earth.

What did this really mean? Slipping off the bed, she gathered her clothes.

"You're not staying?" Miguel gently rubbed her back as Lily pulled up her shorts. Reaching down, she found her hair elastic and lobbed her waves into a quick bun.

"I need to get some sleep, Miguel. I'll see you tomorrow." His confused look made her uneasy, but she needed some time on her own.

CHAPTER SIXTEEN

Pushing the stiff window open, Miguel put down the glass of lemon water after a steady gulp. Flopping onto his bed, he pressed out the wrinkles of the sheet beneath him, still sensing her lavender scent. He had slept alone in the studio for over six months but had never felt it empty—until this very moment.

In his mind, Miguel caressed long chestnut waves. He had never seen Lily's hair so wild and free; she was even more beautiful if that was possible. His smile grew when he recalled her high-pitched pleasure cry that the entire B&B probably heard! What a perfect night.

Now he couldn't sleep. Tossing from side to side, his mind tussled between longing and worry. He just wanted to hold her and fall asleep in their cocoon.

He glanced at his watch again. Pushing the sheets away, Miguel was struck cold by the fact that Lily would be leaving—for good—in a few weeks. His heart sank. Was it wise to get involved, only to see it end so soon? This last year had been brutal. Could he handle another loss?

He flipped to his other side and stared out the window.

The country night sky was pitch black. Lily navigated her room, following the sound of Jade's nasal breathing. Her friend had occupied the entire span of the bed and needed some prodding as Lily slipped in beside her and curled up to the edge.

She could be downstairs, cloaked in Miguel's arms. Why did she bolt? It had been a heavenly night. Those dreamy eyes put her in a trance. His touch made her feel alluring, and uninhibited.

What did it mean? Their argument brought on the heat. Their attraction to each other was obvious, but was this just a hookup? Some twisted victory over Lucas? Her heart passionately disagreed but her head reminded her of Miguel walking away from her at the Caballo Blanco. Besides, she had to keep her head on straight. Lily was returning home soon.

Elena knocked on the door with urgency, as her powerful voice penetrated the wood. "Miguel, do you want *me* to make the coffee? It's a bit late."

Stepping through the door, Miguel tucked his shirt into his jeans, and fastened his belt. "Sorry Elena. I couldn't sleep and just got some shut eye an hour ago." Rubbing his eyes, he let out a loud yawn.

Never one to hold back, Elena pulled him into the hallway. "Did you have company? I thought I heard ... *something* last night." Her eyes widened as her brows lifted in an unnatural way.

"Maybe." Blushing, he felt like a teenager caught kissing the mayor's daughter behind the church.

Elena's broad hand covered her mouth. "I don't know what to say!" She shadowed him into the kitchen, bucket in hand. He tried to escape her questions.

Greeting the Italian brothers at the harvest table, Miguel apologized for his tardiness and got to work. Elena discreetly leaned on the counter, fishing. "So? Who was it?"

Miguel had learned a long time ago that Elena could wear down a veteran MI6 agent. Best to just give in. "Lily Harrison, Elena. Now can I get back to making breakfast?"

"That was quick! You devil!"

"I met her three weeks ago." Clinking as they dropped, the coffee beans came face-to-face with the grinder. Thankfully, the shrill noise of the machine drowned her words.

"You did seem off, yesterday. I guess she must be very special to you?"

The kitchen was charged with the aroma of coffee, as he filled the basket of the moka pot. Unable to contain a spontaneous grin, Miguel nodded.

Pinching his cheek, Elena resumed her duties. "I will hear the full story later."

Laying the ribbons of ham onto the frying pan, he quickly cut the camembert and placed the creamy slices inside the splayed croissants. He looked up at the brothers. "Would you like the breakfast sandwich?"

Camille Morneau had suggested Miguel try the combination, and it was an instant hit with his guests. Preparing the dish, Miguel heard the two Canadian women coming down the staircase. Warmth radiated through his body.

"Good morning, Miguel." Jade's smug face was not unexpected. "I'll take this." Scooping the platter of croissants from the counter, Jade glided over, delivering the breakfast. "Ciao, Stefano e Gabriele!"

Miguel marvelled at Jade's ability to command a room.

His gem trailed behind. Grazing her bare leg as she passed, Miguel brushed her lingering hand, his pulse racing. He whispered in her direction. "Good morning, beautiful." Her smile met her glossy green eyes. The yellow sleeveless dress clung confidently to her delicate curves.

"Let me help you." Lily quickly assembled the tray with the coffee, orange juice pitcher, and water. He felt so at ease when she was around, even when he was paralyzed with panic over Amaya's disappearance.

As Lily found the right cupboard for each required item, Miguel stood transfixed. "Have you visited this kitchen before?"

"Lucky guesses, I suppose." She giggled, hurrying the tray to the eager table.

Miguel watched her join the other guests, feeling like luck had finally knocked on *his* door. Breathing in the fresh valley air, Miguel picked up the phone to make an overdue phone call.

"Antonio … I have been a complete ass. I'm sorry that I ever questioned you. You have always had my back and your friendship means everything to me. Please accept my apology."

Miguel's smile radiated as he put down the handset.

Only in Spain, had red wine been so integral to lesson planning. Fergus filled their glasses, as Charlotte demonstrated how to create a jellyfish from paper plates and crepe "tentacles." Ramón distributed the recipe for Sand Dollar Almond Cookies, while Harper displayed his class set of Ocean Animals Bingo. The giant Octopus Mobile that Ella described was what Lily wanted to start with. Cutting out the shapes of the sea creatures would be slow. Lily shared the picture books she had purchased at Arco Íris, highlighting the ones fitting the theme of "Under the Sea."

Near the end of the day, silliness took over when Julia herded the group for an animated round of Simon Says. Her commands to "chomp like a shark; tiptoe on the hot sand; surf the waves; and dive like a dolphin," were eagerly followed by the tipsy staff. Even the new teachers Fergus had hired fit in perfectly with the spirit of the day camp.

Lily had missed her Alegría colleagues, but her thoughts were lost in Puente La Reina, reviewing every aspect of the last twenty-four hours. Images of the town, Casa Emi, and the night with Miguel twirled in her daydreams as she cut the construction paper. Was it a one-night stand? Did Miguel care about her? Was he even back in Pamplona?

Fergus entered the classroom, toting a box of baby food jars, sand, and tempera paint. "Here you go, Lily. If you have time early next week, the Sand Jar craft is popular with the wee ones."

"Good idea. I have extra sidewalk chalk if any of the other teachers are doing the Sea Life Mural."

Fergus flopped by Lily on the carpeted floor of the Reading Corner. It was unusual to see Fergus so tired.

"I'm wiped. Please remind me to get more sleep, love."

As he spoke, Lily hoped for the complete opposite.

Fergus put his arm around her, playfully swaying her body. "Did you enjoy Puente La Reina?"

Pushing him away, Lily beamed. "You know I did, Fergus." She assumed having a brother must feel like this.

Squinting, he rubbed his chin. "So, I can put you back on yard duty in the morning?" His kindness towards her was comforting.

As she spoke, Lily swung her scissors like a conductor's baton. "Yes, Fergus. Thank you. I won't be avoiding Miguel anymore—but I'm sure Jade has already filled you in!"

"Of course, she did. She was rather proud of the success of her scheme."

The two chuckled, sharing a knowing smile. "That sounds like Jade. She called herself the architect of my joy!" Their laughter continued.

"Seriously, lass. Jade wanted to find a way to thank you for bringing the two of us together, so she arranged the getaway." Fergus spoke in a quiet voice. His eyes were soft.

"I don't deserve credit, Fergus. She introduced me to you, remember?"

"Yes, but you invited her to Pamplona."

Lily pursed her lips, not entirely convinced.

"Jade absolutely adores you and wants you to be happy, darling." Fergus rubbed his tired eyes and strolled to the door. "Now, if you will excuse me, I need to check out the back of the school. Claudia says she saw a man with a banged-up face lurking around out there."

It was a perfect summer day. The sun was bright but not sizzling. A wispy breeze waded through the oak trees lining the inn. Miguel took in the serenity of the countryside. He struggled to recall the last time he felt so peaceful. Lily's moss-green eyes tinted his daydream, as he walked outside.

"Gracias, Javier." Waving goodbye, as the white truck reversed out of the driveway, Miguel was pleased with the bathroom handrail installation. Convinced Isabel's recovery would be accelerated at Casa Emi, a lightness filled his chest. His plans were slowly coming together.

Elena bellowed from the window, "Can you give me a hand here?" Miguel realized she required no help, only information on Señorita Harrison! He needed a favour from her, so ducking her request was not an option.

Fresh wildflowers crowded the vase resting on the dresser Elena was dusting. The blue quilt pooled on the armchair. Miguel bit his lip. "*You* need help making the bed?"

"That would be nice." Her innocent demeanour did not fool him.

"I wanted to give you this." Elena indicated with her sharp chin and Miguel instantly spotted a familiar, well-worn pair of Converse beside the wall. "I think your … friend … forgot them. The blonde one would never wear this style of shoe."

"True. They are Lily's." He couldn't contain his smile. The sneakers, in some ways, resembled Lily: beautiful in design, practical, and resilient. "I'll take them to her tomorrow night. Which reminds me … I need to ask a favour. Could you stay Wednesday night?"

Elena ignored his question and stuck to her agenda. "So, tell me about her. I must give Cristina an update." She launched the fitted sheet his way, the scent of roses hovered.

Taking a step back, he tucked the sheet into the corner of the bed. "My mother? Why an update?"

"I called her yesterday to tell her Lily was here. What an incredible coincidence that she should know your mother!" Miguel nodded. He still found the connection unbelievable. "I promised her I would introduce the two of you." Smoothing out the wrinkles, Elena lofted the flat sheet his way, as she chuckled. "But clearly, no introduction was needed."

A relaxed grin crossed his face. "Correct." Stuffing the pillows into the shams, Miguel said nothing, unnerving his curious friend.

"Okay, you can remain silent, but I already know a great deal about Lily." Elena yanked the quilt from the chair and laid it on the bed.

She was skillful in the art of probing. "Like what?" Miguel was drawn in.

After throwing the decorative pillows on the bed, Elena sat in the armchair and stretched her arms above her head. "Let's make this interesting. I'll tell you what I know if you answer a few questions."

Miguel knew he was descending into a rabbit hole. "And if I refuse?"

"You want me to stay tomorrow tonight, don't you?"

Surrendering, Miguel sat on the warm wood floor, leaning against the bed, face-to-face with his interrogator.

Elena clasped her hands together as she reported. "According to Cristina, Lily is an incredible person. She is pretty, athletic, intelligent, kind, and sensitive." *This, and so much more.* "She lost her father recently and was sadly abandoned by her mother as a child. While in Pamplona, she met a wonderful and complicated man— you—who didn't treat her well. Shameful! Cristina also suspects it was Lily who suggested that Amaya see Isabel. Great advice! When she returns to Canada, she will be looking for a new apartment, and starting a permanent teaching job." He was stunned to hear how much personal information had been shared between the women and equally wounded to learn about Lily's plans for the future … far from him.

The telephone rang as Elena was finishing. "Oh … also, she is a wonderful baker. Now it's your turn."

"I'll be right back." He darted downstairs to the mahogany desk to answer the phone.

"Miguel?"

It was Cristina, no doubt impatient to be briefed by Elena. As he listened, his shoulders slumped, and a wave of nausea told hold. Her news shattered his peace.

CHAPTER SEVENTEEN

Grateful to have napped after school, Lily felt refreshed, and impatient to see Miguel. She had missed him yesterday. Rushing to leave her pensión, Lily grabbed her Pops's red pañuelo.

The streets were quiet, as many tourists had already left the city. Crossing in front of a man leaning into the shoe shop entrance, Lily wondered why his sky-blue baseball cap was pulled over his eyes. Journeying towards the Plaza del Castillo, Lily thought this man looked familiar.

Lily straightened her red scarf over her white shirt, one last time. The festival uniform would be retired tonight, after the Pobre de Mí, or "Poor Me" send off, in the City Hall square. An eighties tribute-band performed a rendition of "Wake Me Up Before You Go-Go," as the crowd danced. After nine glorious days, the San Fermín festival would soon end, and her father's wish would be fulfilled. A soft wave of satisfaction washed over her.

Battling through the crowd, she spotted Jade, and Beatriz beneath the pale white awning of the Café Iruña.

"¡Hola, chicas!" Two hardy embraces were exchanged. "Where is everyone?"

Jade tapped the patio chair beside her. Lily took her spot. "Fergus is under the weather and Antonio and Miguel are coming shortly."

"He wasn't his usual energetic self at school." She recognized the disappointment in Jade's eyes. With only two full days left before returning home, Lily imagined every moment Jade spent with Fergus was precious especially since he was working full-time.

A gin and tonic awaited her at the table. "Thanks for this! I overslept."

Sneering at Bea, Jade bounced back. "Are you catching up on the lost sleep from our stay at Puente?" The three highball glasses clinked in celebration, followed by laughter.

Bea reached for Lily's hand. "I'm happy for you two. *This* is the Miguel I know. You've done the impossible and brought him back to life!"

"I like *this* Miguel, muchísimo." Popping a handful of almonds, Lily relaxed into the chair. Another gulp of the refreshing drink washed the saltiness.

"I am visiting Ochagavía with Jade tomorrow. I think it's the most enchanting town in this province." In Lily's mind, Puente La Reina would be tough to beat. "My aunt will prepare a delicious lunch for us."

Rubbing her hands together, Jade's excitement was clear. "While the rest of you labour, *I'll* be taking in the pure air of the Pyrenees." Bea raised her glass to Jade and finished her drink.

"You and Miguel can come on the weekend. He's been countless times."

Lily basked in the sound of *you and Miguel*. "Great idea."

Antonio headed for the table, candles in hand. Her chest tightened to see him alone. "Hello, everyone." Kissing Bea sweetly, he remained standing, focussing on Lily. "Miguel is on his way. He had to go to the hospital—all I know is Isabel fell during her physiotherapy session."

"This is upsetting! She was doing so well when I visited yesterday." Bea's sorrowful eyes reflected the mood of the table.

"Let's stay positive, amor." He stroked Bea's arm and signalled the women to follow him.

Nudging their way through the crush of people, Antonio led them to the meeting spot beneath the Gutierrez Clothing store sign. The evening air was cool, bringing some relief to the jammed bodies in the square. The sombre participants held lit candles in plastic cups, flickering in the darkness of midnight.

The mayor's words closed the festival from the balcony of the City Hall, one of Lily's favourite buildings in the Old Town. She felt confident, like the baroque sculpture above that featured a woman playing a golden trumpet.

Removing the pañuelo until next July was part of this ceremony. A hand gripped her shoulder as she untied the knot in her father's red scarf. "Miguel!"

The crowd erupted into the mournful tune, "Pobre de Mí," accompanied by the band. The square was adorned with scarves extended overhead and the softness of candlelight, as the locals and visitors lamented the end of the festivities.

Miguel's embrace was loose. As he leaned to kiss the top of her head, Lily's lips felt abandoned.

"I'm sorry about Isabel." Too noisy to talk, Lily joined the crowd, swaying as she sang, while securing the candle and scarf. Miguel's serious face had returned, and she feared it had little to do with saying goodbye to San Fermín.

The fireworks cascaded, as Miguel folded his scarf, and handed it to Lily. "I want you to have this." She smiled at his pensive face that screened the colours of the illuminations above.

Clutching the scarf to her heart, her eyes thanked him, and the knots in her stomach loosened.

Pacing to his car after the fireworks, Lily set out to hold Miguel's hand but settled for linked fingers.

"I'm sorry about Isabel. What happened?" Freed of the crowd and noise, the distance between them was obvious.

Speaking slowly, he stared at the sidewalk. "She fell … and dislocated her hip at physio, today. She may need surgery."

Lily grimaced. *Poor woman.* "How is she feeling?"

Miguel unlocked the hatchback, pulling out a plastic bag. "She was in a lot of pain today, and we didn't really talk. Amaya called from her father's place, but Isa was asleep."

Elevating his mood was impossible. "She'll be stronger tomorrow. This just happened today, Miguel."

He passed Lily the parcel. "You forgot your sneakers." A flash of comfort skipped through her chest, thinking about the B&B.

Looking into the bag, her free hand rested on her chest. "I have a lot of history with these guys. Thank you!" Miguel sloped against the passenger door of his silver car. Lily leaned into him, positioning her lips in his direction. With both hands, he gently pushed her shoulders away.

Her stomach sank at the rejection. Watching him pull out the beat-up cigarette pack, Lily swallowed hard. The streetlamp lit his gloomy face. "What's going on? Can we talk at my pensión? It's on this street."

Looking away, he didn't move. "I don't think that's a good idea."

What is happening? A painful tightness took over her throat. Leaning against the car door beside him, Lily nervously rocked the plastic bag.

He spoke in a controlled whisper. "My life is too chaotic, Lily … I had foolishly counted on Isa coming home next week and my mother changing her mind about selling the B&B. It's all ruined now! My sister has suffered a serious setback, and the hospital bills continue to grow. There is no way to delay the sale of my grandparent's house, now. Things never seem to work out the way they should."

Lily slipped her hand into his and brought it to her lips. "I'm so sorry, Miguel. How can I help?"

Sharply pulling his hand back, Lily froze.

His eyes were glued on his fidgeting hands. "I need you to walk away from me and say goodbye."

Miguel's words pommelled her. Shock spiralled, deep inside. Silent, Lily measured her options. Her voice trembled when she finally spoke. "Is this what you really want?"

Miguel did not reply.

In the silence, the sting of Miguel's words mingled with anger. She turned to face him, lifting his downcast head. "I know what you are doing, Miguel. You feel overwhelmed and want to protect yourself by pushing me away." Lily lost herself in his widening sad eyes.

"What if I am?"

Fighting tears, Lily spoke directly. "Then you are not the person I thought you were. Things get tough, and your solution is to just let me go." Her chin trembled as the colour drained from her cheeks. *Just like Véronique.*

"Will I not have to let you go anyway, in a few weeks? Your life is six-thousand kilometres away from me, Lily." Pain flushed through his face.

Picking up the bag, resignation burned through her dull eyes. "What hurts most is you don't care enough to try and see where this goes. If we are meant to be together, *we* can find a way. But *you* have already quit. I was a fool to believe this might actually work." She kissed his cheek and walked quickly down her street. "Goodbye, Miguel."

Dashing towards the pensión, Lily had a gut feeling she was being followed. Was Miguel pursuing her, hoping to clear up their misunderstanding? He had hurt her for the last time—she could not give him the satisfaction of turning her head. By the time she entered the lobby alone, the eerie feeling had stopped.

"What a surprise! I didn't expect you home, tonight." Cristina sat at the kitchen table reviewing the realtor's file. Her reading glasses slid along her broad nose, as Miguel greeted his mother with a kiss. Casting open the refrigerator door, he avoided eye contact.

"My plans changed." Filling the glass with water, his hand shook. He could feel her eyes inspecting him.

Rubbing her temples, she lifted her terracotta mug of camomile tea. "What's wrong? You look awful."

"I don't want to talk about it, Mamá." Miguel swallowed the water, dampening his dry throat. He turned to her, certain his mother had spotted his red eyes. He had made the right decision, but the wreckage it had left behind, devastated him. Lily's vacant eyes, as she walked away, remained imprinted.

"Did you have an argument with Lily?"

He shook his head, hoping the movement would remove the image of her pained face. Hurting her again ... was unforgivable.

"Look—I told her I couldn't see her anymore." Pinching the bridge of his nose, Miguel closed his eyes. "I'm a mess, Mamá. She deserves better. I'm going to bed."

His heavy feet dragged along the hall, as his mother spoke after him. "She *does* deserve better ... but she wants *you*—you stubborn fool! You are throwing away a rare experience in this life, my boy."

Entering her room, a gush of tears exploded, relieving the accumulated heat in Lily's eyes. Face first, she collapsed on her bed and steadied her breathing. Pulling the red scarf from her back pocket, she held it to her lips. She was in love with a man who had asked her to walk away. *How could he let me go so easily?* It felt like a cruel pattern, woven deep into her life. She lay there, clutching the scarf, for over an hour, unscrambling the clutter.

Vaulting off the bed, she grabbed her overnight bag from the chair, still packed from Puente La Reina. Organizing it with fresh clothes, she prepared to leave. Being alone tonight was not possible.

Lily changed out of her white jeans and top—her decision was made. The bag draped over her slumped shoulder as she wandered to La Perla, sorting out the details of her plan. She had to quit this cruel rollercoaster ride.

The Plaza del Castillo seemed quiet tonight. Tomorrow would see more tourists departing and locals resuming their usual lives. While counting down the days to July 6, 2011, the city would be cleansed of this year's celebration and return to normalcy. *A new beginning for everyone.*

Lily patted her eyes as she rode the elevator. The puffiness had subsided, and her headache was now under control. Jade opened the door with a sage green eye mask resting on her forehead, holding back her tangled hair.

"Lily?"

"I'm going back with you. On Saturday."

CHAPTER EIGHTEEN

Lily had slept soundly at La Perla and woke up with energy to burn. It felt soothing to jog on the sidewalks of the freshly washed streets. Her pace was quick, hurrying her run to make time for a luxurious shower in Jade's studio. She would have the large washroom to herself, as Bea had already picked up Jade for their adventure in the Irati forest.

Lily felt calmer, but a strange numbness had set in. Unaware of her surroundings, she did not see Lucas standing across the street. Concentrating only on essential tasks was the plan to occupy her wandering mind. Her belly knotted, as she approached her first stop at the café. She couldn't leave without saying goodbye to Cristina.

Lily held the scallop shell in her sweaty hand … it now seemed ridiculous to give Cristina a souvenir from her own hometown. The patio tables and chairs had not been arranged, but the sparkling droplets of water on the irises meant Cristina must be around.

The sign above the magenta door now made sense: Café Miisa. A glum smile emerged as she discovered the combined names of Cristina's two beloved children.

Looking around for the owner, Lily spotted a white envelope with her name on it, hung by the Closed sign. She nervously drew out the monogrammed piece of paper containing a farewell letter. The café would be closed for a few weeks and Cristina wanted to say goodbye. She included her telephone number and encouraged

Lily to keep in touch. "Tu eres muy especiale, Lily." Lily's eyes welled, already missing this affectionate woman who had shown her so much kindness.

Before leaving, Lily looped the red yarn securing the Camino shell around the knob of the café door. Cristina would know who had left it there.

What direction would Lily's own camino take? She had much to think about as she jogged back to the hotel.

Stepping into the speckled shower stall, the discussion with herself continued.

Lucas sat on the copper-coloured bench facing La Perla.

Knowing the boss had its perks—it certainly made breaking the contract at Alegría, uncomplicated. Lily had never quit a job this way and the guilt set in. Her father had taught her to follow through on a commitment. She had persisted, even with jobs she hated, like the stint delivering pizza, or the summer as a telemarketer. This was ... different. She adored everything about the school but remaining in Spain was not possible.

Clipboard in hand, Fergus gripped a football under his arm. He was a giant beside the dancing campers in the front yard. "Alvaro, you are in charge, pal. Include everyone." He lobbed the ball and stepped aside, avoiding the stampede of little people.

"You look rested." His tight embrace gave her goosebumps. The loss of her Alegría colleagues and students chiselled another hole in her heart.

They strolled across the small field to his office. "I'm feeling much better today. How are you, lass?"

Lily shrugged her shoulders, as she looked away. Switching on her sunny voice, she replied, "I'll be better when I get home and occupy myself with finding a new apartment and setting up my classroom for the fall." This idea of her future had always carried a burst of excitement. Today, she felt nothing.

"I'm glad to hear it, love. Trevor will be taking your classes today, so you can bring Silvia up to speed. She is no Lily, but I think she'll fit in nicely."

A tear rolled down her cheek as Lily stroked his sturdy arm. "I can't thank you enough, Fergus. You have treated me like family." Collecting herself, she pushed the lump in her throat. "I'll return your kindness when you come visit Toronto." He winked at her, nodding, as a broad smile hijacked his face.

Knocking, Claudia popped her head in. "So sorry to interrupt. Trevor would like you to talk to Amaya, Lily. She seems upset about you leaving." Saying goodbye to Amaya would be another bruising aspect of her day. "She is outside."

"Go, Lil. You can meet Silvia later, in the staff room. I'll let her know."

Letting out a hard sigh, Lily closed her eyes briefly as she entered the bright hallway. Amaya ran to her, clinging to her waist. "¿Es cierto que te vas? I don't want you to go, Miss Harrison." Hunching, Lily held the girl's hands firmly. Amaya lowered her head, hiding her tears, as she parked herself against the cinderblock wall.

"I am leaving, sweetheart, and I will miss you so much. This makes me feel sad too." Amaya looked at her, wiping the tears from her rosy cheeks.

"I was hoping you could do me a big favour?" Reaching into her backpack, Lily set a violet box on the girl's lap. Amaya lifted the lid, running her fingers over the pretty writing paper. "I printed my temporary address on three envelopes. I would be so happy if you would write to me. You can practice your English and send me your beautiful drawings." The child's face brightened.

"Will you come back?" Amaya's chocolate brown eyes were like Miguel's. Lily's chest tightened.

Blanketing her in a hug, Lily responded, "Maybe." Amaya giggled as Lily helped her up.

"I'll write to you, Miss Harrison." Feeling at ease, Lily secured Amaya's hand and skipped along the hall.

"I'll take you back to class."

"Flowers! How thoughtful, Miguel." Pressing the button on the side of the bed, Isabel shifted to an upright position. Her cheeks had colour and her mood was jovial. Amaya's drawings decorated the sterile white wall behind the bed.

"I picked them this morning, from the yard. The purple foxgloves have taken over." He kissed his sister's forehead and pulled the armchair closer to her. "A little reminder of home, while we still have it." Miguel instantly regretted his comment. His sister saw the alarm on his face.

"It breaks my heart to lose Casa Emi, but it's Mamá's decision to make. Other opportunities will present themselves." Isa's calm puzzled him. This was not the reaction he expected. "Stop fighting her over this, Miguel."

"I thought you would be so upset!"

"I'm choosing to focus on what really counts." The tension that had clung to Miguel's chest for weeks, melted.

Placing the small vase on her overbed table, he noticed the half-eaten dark chocolate bar. "I see Antonio has been here!"

Her giddiness was infectious. "He spoils me."

"We are all so relieved that you don't need surgery." He squeezed her hand gently. "You'll have to stay here a bit longer, though." A bitter smile emerged, as he leaned back.

"I can handle it, Miguel. I can get through anything, with the support of people who love me. Especially my little champion, Amaya."

Miguel's muscles relaxed into the metal chair. Isabel's old self had re-emerged.

Holding Miguel's hand, she swung their arms like they were kids again. "My therapist suggested I share a story with you. I think it can help you, too."

Keen to hear, Miguel straightened.

"Two days ago, Susana's mother came to see me for the first time." His stomach tightened, as he forced a fake smile. "She appreciated seeing you at the cemetery." Miguel's tears surfaced, as his sister spoke.

"You can imagine how emotional the visit was. Before she left, she had me promise I wouldn't blame myself for the accident—nor feel guilty I survived." Droplets streamed down her cheeks. Miguel handed her a tissue and breathed in deeply.

"You blamed yourself for the accident?"

Isa's lips trembled as she reached out her hand. "I guess I did, on some level. In the same way I think you blame *yourself*, Miguel. You must let it go ... or it will consume you."

He had intimate knowledge of this power. The thought of letting it go brought some relief.

Isabel blew her nose and grabbed the chocolate, snapping off a piece. "This treat cures everything!"

"And you're not sharing?!" Their laughter brightened the moment.

Rubbing her hands together, she now encouraged Miguel to share. "Tell me about this Miss Harrison. Amaya adores her."

"Not much to tell. I've ruined things between us." His confidante was back, and Miguel needed her insight.

Pub Karaoke was the ideal spot for Lily's farewell on her last day at school. Little time would be left to question her decision to leave Pamplona, as her colleagues sang on stage. Pablo was the first with an impressive "Gasolina." He warmed the crowd with the Daddy Yankee classic.

The walls were covered with random movie posters, ads for San Miguel Cerveza, and license plates. The smell of ale and sweat floated to the beams of yellow light, rotating in a circular motion from the disco ball. Cheap metal stools lined the dented wooden counter. Framed by metallic fringe curtains, the modest stage occupied the back of the bar.

Mateo recruited Lily to join him for a raucous, "I Will Survive," as Jade, Bea, and Antonio entered. Jumping off the stage, Lily wiped the moisture from her forehead and thanked her colleague with a sticky embrace. Fergus handed her another beer, as she kissed the newcomers.

"How was Ochagavía?" Antonio's arm remained locked over Lily's shoulders.

Looking uncomfortable as she settled onto the red stool, Jade threw her arms wide. "Absolutely picturesque."

Charlotte waved at them as she chose, "Girls Just Want to Have Fun." Bea and Jade disappeared into the spotlight.

"I'm disappointed you are leaving." Antonio's sincere eyes were tinted with concern. This was precisely the type of conversation Lily needed to avoid.

"Me too." Swallowing, she applauded the women on stage.

"I'm guessing I can't change your mind?"

Lily longed for a reason to stay, but she knew it didn't exist. She shook her head and Antonio released his arm.

"Okay, I understand."

Fergus dove between them. "Don't be bringing down my girl, Antonio. This is a celebration!" The three of them howled.

How would she function without her Scottish bodyguard or her Spanish confidantes? Scanning the bar, Lily was surrounded by love. It had been a remarkable trip. *Thanks, Pops.*

CHAPTER NINETEEN

The front yard of the school buzzed with childhood joy, on that grey Friday morning. A few parents chatted by the sidewalk, as their sons, and daughters danced around them. It was overcast, but the threat of rain did not diminish the positive energy.

Miguel waved at Amaya, as she joined her friends in a round of Double Dutch. Claudia, the student monitor, kept an eye on the kids, while Fergus made his rounds, shaking little hands, and kicking balls. Miguel recognized a few of the teachers, strolling through the field, but he didn't see her.

Maybe this was a mistake. He had no right to ask Lily for another chance. He didn't deserve it, but Miguel trusted his sister's advice. Isa understood him like no one else.

Lighter, he inhaled deeply, calming the nerves settling in his stomach. He walked towards the entrance; light raindrops following him. "Buenos días, Fergus. Could you tell me Lily's room number?"

Rubbing his chin, Fergus stepped back. "Lily's last day with us was yesterday, Miguel. She's returning home tomorrow, with Jade."

A sudden feeling of cold expanded from his core, stiffening every muscle. Ramming his eyes shut, his heart rapidly palpitated. *No ... this can't be happening.*

"I'm sorry, man." Fergus patted his back. "Did you want to come in?"

Shaking his head, he darted back to his car.

Lily had carved out a free afternoon. Her laundry was dry and most of the packing was done. Tucking Miguel's red scarf into the mesh pocket of the luggage made it very real. Forgetting him would be a challenge. Cut short, her dream vacation was over.

Needing to unwind, Lily threaded the laces of her running shoes. The rhythm of her foot strikes, combined with her firm heartbeat, smoothed out the difficult times. Jogging started each day, a lifeline since her first run as a child—when Pops told her Véronique would not be coming back.

The Taconera Park with its majestic trees and vibrant flowers was the oasis she craved, despite the light rain. Lily headed out, unable to shake the feeling that she was being followed, wishing it might be Miguel.

Crossing the stately entrance of San Nicolás reminded Lily of photographs of the Arc de Triomphe in Paris. The whole park, with its manicured gardens, was very "Versailles-esque". Given her financial state, this might be the closest she would get to France in some time. Could the post-vacation blues already be crowding her head?

Be in the moment, Lily. She picked up the pace on the damp gravel trail, her negative thoughts temporarily broken by the song of birds nearby and squirrels playing hide and go seek. Just minutes away from the narrow streets of the Old Town and yet this park was so tranquil.

Pamplonicas of all ages shared this urban gem. Lily surveyed couples strolling, teenagers picnicking, families cycling together, and many dog walkers enjoying the cool shade. The panoramic views of the city with the adjoining Pyrenees, forged a precious postcard in her mind.

Stopping by the railing overlooking the mini-zoo, Lily shared the view with a group of children. Complete with a moat and framed by the city's original wall, peacocks, roosters, ducks, geese, swans, chickens, and deer roamed freely. Lily shared a laugh with the children as they imitated the clucking of the geese.

Feeling calmer, she was about to resume her jog. That's when she spotted the man with the sky-blue baseball cap walking towards her.

"Lucas?"

Arco Íris Bookstore was a short drive from the school but felt like a world away to Miguel. He held his forehead, his flushed skin moist with sweat, and raindrops. "Why didn't you tell me she was leaving?"

Throwing his hands, Antonio pinched his lips together. "Why would I tell you, Miguel? For once, I didn't interfere. Isn't it enough that I fired my cousin for you?"

Squeezing his hands until his knuckles turned white, Miguel's head pounded. "I wish you had! I must talk to her, Antonio—I need to see her ... I can't believe I don't have her number!"

"Let me call Jade."

Miguel nervously paced around the book stacks to burn off his rigid tension.

Shaking his head, Antonio put down the handset. "She's not answering—but I left her a message. Stay calm, Miguel. You'll find her."

His voice was hoarse and shaky. "Yes ... you're right. I'll check the pensión and La Perla. She must be there."

Antonio's level head and embrace eased his best friend's queasiness. "Good luck, Miguel. Keep me posted."

Lucas removed his cap, running a hand through his hair. His tense lips curled as he spoke. "Hello, Lily."

Smoothing down her T-shirt, she stepped back, watching the children skip away to another section of the park. *Had he followed her?* "What a surprise, Lucas. How are you?" Faking a sunny mood was her first instinct.

Placing a steady hand on her shoulder, Lucas guided Lily along the railing. "Let me show you a spectacular view of the city's ancient wall." His voice was serious but not unfriendly. *Maybe running into Lucas was just a coincidence.*

Glancing around, Lily trudged, her stomach a knot of heaviness. This peaceful park now felt menacing. Lucas stopped under an overgrown tree-lined path. As it turns out, the Taconera also had many hidden corners and dark pockets. Lily gripped the railing with both hands, breathing deeply as Lucas's overly confident touch burned into her shoulder.

Miguel drove around Pamplona for hours, desperately looking for Lily. Antonio had still not heard from Jade. The pensión receptionist hadn't seen Lily all day and the stuffy concierge at La Perla confirmed that Ms. Allen was also not in her room.

His heartbeat echoed in his throat, his limbs tingling with fatigue. She could be anywhere and finding her now was impossible. Tomorrow, she would be gone. Pain shot through his body like a summer wildfire.

Gripping the steering wheel and wishing for another miracle, Miguel turned around and headed for the Bodegón, where they had first met over spilled beer.

Cracking his neck from side to side, Lucas stared at her without blinking. "I'm doing better than the last time we saw each other."

Lily's breath was shallow as she babbled, "I'm glad. That was an ugly situation, Lucas."

Holding his chin up, his voice deepened. "I agree. I found it ugly that you abandoned me on our date and left with Miguel—after he *attacked* me."

"But Amaya was missing! I *had* to help him." Lily's chin trembled as a pearl of sweat rolled down her cheek. Frantically scanning the formerly busy area, she now saw no one.

Lucas's voice thundered, "What are you talking about?? Are you lying to me?!!"

"No, Lucas. Amaya went missing and I stayed to help Miguel find her." Lily cleared her throat and tried to step away from his hold—he seemed to be unravelling.

"I don't believe you." He clenched Lily's wrist, squeezing it hard. "You all LIE. Susana and I were *finally* together … and then she dropped me—to try to win Miguel back. You are just like her, Lily."

Overtaken by panic, Lily's heart palpitated. Reaching for her phone, she tugged her arm away. She had to call Jade. Lily spoke quickly as she fumbled with her phone. *Pick up Jade. Pick up. Please.* "Listen, Lucas, I'm sorry that you are so upset but I never lied to you—"

Pulling herself away from him, Lily dropped her phone. Lucas kicked it between the railing, launching it to the grass of the enclosed area metres below. Adrenaline raced through Lily's veins. With a strength she never knew she owned; she rushed Lucas. Slipping on the wet gravel, he stumbled and fell, allowing Lily to flee.

Clubbing his head on the stone edging of the flower bed, Lucas lay motionless. Glancing back, Lily's leg muscles were trembling, but she would not stop running. She needed to get to safety. Sprinting, San Nicolás street was near, and Dani was always at the Bodegón. He would help her.

CHAPTER TWENTY

With his shoulders pulled low, Dani's heavy arms wrung out the bar towel. "I haven't seen her since the final match. I'm sorry Miguel."

Slumping into the chair, he hauled out the crushed Marlboro pack and threw it on the bar. "Take this away, Dani—I'm about to light one."

The older man's piercing eyes witnessed his friend's pain. "Let me fix you a drink."

Mental fatigue had set in. Miguel had no new plan. "No thanks. I think I need to take a walk and clear my head. If Antonio comes by, tell him to wait for me."

Devoid of energy, Miguel drifted out the door. Rubbing his aching eyes, he was unprepared to be thumped by her charging body, barrelling around the corner. "*Lily!*"

Her entire body shook, her face was colourless, and she was making no sense. "I don't think he was moving . . . but I kept running, just in case he got up, and followed me again!"

"Lily! What happened?!" Miguel steadied her shoulders with his hands but her head continued to rock back and forth as she tried to catch her breath.

Lily moved forward, squeezing her eyes shut. "Lucas has been following me." The jolt charged through Miguel's entire body. "He confronted me at La Taconera—freaking out about how I had abandoned him—like Susana had." Miguel's heart sank. His worries about Lucas had panned out.

Lifting Lily's arm, Miguel noticed the marks on her wrist. "He kicked away my phone when I tried to call Jade." Miguel pulled Lily into an embrace; stroking the back of her head, he tried to lull her panic.

"I'm so sorry. Just breathe, Lily."

Her terrified face looked up at him. "I pushed him away, Miguel, and ran … I think he slipped and hit his head."

Miguel's fingers tingled as he worked out a plan. "Where did this happen? I can go see what's happening and call 112 if he is hurt. You should stay here, with Dani. You're in shock, Lily."

"No—I'm coming with you, Miguel." She took his hand, and they walked in silence as Lily tried to steady her breathing.

"Thank you, Señorita Harrison. That is all." The stern-faced police officer gathered up his paperwork and left the office. His friendlier colleague confirmed that Lucas had regained consciousness. Lily pressed her palms into her eyes. A swell of relief filled her chest.

"Thanks for staying with me, Miguel." His presence had kept her grounded and safe.

Nodding, his eyes glowed. "Of course—just returning the favour." His wink disarmed the tension. Scanning the familiar sterile office, Lily laughed.

"Who knew my vacation would involve so many visits to this police station?"

Miguel chuckled as he stood and leaned on the beige desk, facing her. Their gaze held for some time before Miguel cleared his throat. He spoke slowly. "I wanted to tell you how sorry I am for hurting you, Lily."

Instantly overcome by emotion, Lily didn't hold back. She would be gone tomorrow and needed to soothe the bruise. "Okay,

Miguel ... but this is hard for me. You gave up on me! That pain runs deep." A tear rolled across her cheek.

Miguel inched closer, his watery eyes staring at her with intensity. "I never gave up on *you*, Lily—I gave up on me. I didn't think I deserved to be happy."

"That doesn't really change what happened, Miguel. You asked me to walk away." Anguish spread across Miguel's face, as his chin quivered. He took hold of her hands, perched on her lap. She didn't resist.

"I went to find you this morning at school. I was hoping to talk. To spend whatever time we had, together. When Fergus told me you were leaving, my world crashed." He swallowed hard, tears outlining his sharp cheekbones. "I looked everywhere for you. The thought of never seeing you again shattered me."

Lily shared that pain. She fought back her tears as she listened.

Miguel caressed her cheek and raised her face to his. "I don't want to be without you ... you have invited joy back into my life, even during this chaos."

She couldn't breathe nor speak. He seemed different ... at peace with himself.

Miguel got closer, leaning his forehead on Lily's. Her stomach fluttered as his breath swept her face. "I know I don't deserve you, but I love you, Lily Harrison, and I'm *never* going to give up on us, again. I will earn your trust."

There were no walls left to protect her, just a quiet confidence that she believed in him. Floating, she pulled him in, her lips melting on his full mouth. "I love you too, cariño. I want to somehow make this work." Lily twirled the shell charm on her silver bracelet.

"Maybe I can change my flight again and stay for a few more weeks?" Miguel's finger tenderly traced circles on her cheek, his face beaming.

"I hear there's a cute B&B in Puente La Reina. You should check it out." She kissed him again. "And I'll renew my passport—I have always wanted to visit Toronto."

Lily was now glued to Miguel's adoring eyes. Wrapping his arms around her waist, he passionately drew her close. Her arms closed in around his neck. Lost in his chocolate brown eyes, she couldn't see the entire path forward ... but Lily knew she could live with any ambiguity—as long as it included Miguel.

¡*Buen camino*!

ABOUT THE AUTHOR

Yolanda Elso-Ponzo was born in Pamplona, Spain, and has lived most of her life in Toronto, Canada. She has been privileged to work in the education sector. In her free time, travel, reading, yoga, history, and walking bring Yolanda much joy, as does spending time with her family and friends. *Camino to Love* was written during the isolation of the COVID-19 lockdowns, providing a beautiful escape. This is Yolanda's first novella.

Manufactured by Amazon.ca
Bolton, ON